GONE WITH THE WITCH

TEEN Witch

#3

GONE WITH THE WITCH

MEGAN BARNES

SCHOLASTIC INC.
New York Toronto London Auckland Sydney

ISBN 0-590-41298-1

12 11 10 9 8 7 6 5 4 3 2 1   9/8 0 1 2 3 4/9

Printed in the U.S.A.   01

First Scholastic printing, February 1989

GONE WITH THE WITCH

Chapter 1

"Just because *your* room looks like a tornado swept through it doesn't mean you have any right to turn *mine* into a disaster area, Sarah!" Nicole Connell, her blue eyes stormy, stood tensely in the doorway of her younger sister's bedroom. "If I ever let you wear any of my clothes again, it'll be when you've learned to return them neatly pressed and on hangers, not thrown in a ball on the bed!"

"Sorry, Nicole. I meant to hang them up, but then I heard the phone ringing and, thinking it might be the most gorgeous guy in all of Waterview calling *you* for a date, I naturally dropped everyth — "

"You infant!" Tossing the words over her shoulder as her blunt-cut pageboy flew around her face, Nicole stalked off.

Sarah shrugged, looking down at her cat, Bandit, who lay curled in her lap as she slouched against the wicker headboard of her bed. "It's not easy having a sister who's a prima donna, is it, Bandit?"

"You could at least *try* to get along better with Nicole." Sarah's best friend — not just in Waterview High but in the whole world — spoke calmly but firmly from where she was perched at the foot of the bed.

Ignoring Sarah's weary nod, Micki Davis continued, "Honestly, if I had such a neat family, I'd never take a single one of them for granted. At least Nicole is beautiful and I'd love to have an older brother as cool as Simon! And your folks. . . . Why, your dad's so open and so much fun, no one would suspect he's the most respected pediatrician in the whole town. And to have a mother who's a guidance counselor and understands all your problems!"

"C'mon, now you're making me feel guilty!" Sarah laughed. "As if I'm the Eddie Haskell who's making life miserable for the Cleavers."

"I don't mean to get on your case," Micki said apologetically. "But if you changed places with me for a while — with a father who lives two states away — you'd start taking better care of your sister's clothes."

"Oh, Micki, I know they're all great, and I love them all!" Sarah said warmly, knowing how much Micki would have given to have a big family. "But, honestly, there's no making Nicole happy sometimes. Nobody's as neat as she is, except maybe an operating room nurse. I mean, she even folds her underwear and keeps it arranged in her drawer by color! And her lipsticks! She's got them lined up on top of her bureau like little toy soldiers — in order — from the palest to the deepest shades! Can you believe it?"

"There's nothing wrong with being neat, Sarah," Micki lectured, but a giggle escaped all the same.

Now Sarah laughed, too. "To hear Nicole, you'd think I'd borrowed one of her best outfits instead of an old pair of jeans and a ratty UCLA sweatshirt. And you know I'd never do *that*. I've got too much fashion sense to want to wear any of Ms. Conservative's pastel sweaters and tailored slacks. She dresses like a walking PTA meeting!"

"You certainly do have your own inimitable style," Micki agreed, her brown eyes twinkling as they took in Sarah's present outfit, tight gray cotton leggings and slouch socks, topped by what had been one of Dr. Connell's old white dress shirts, before his daughter had studded it with rhinestones and sewn on tassels.

"Why, even a photo of one of Nicole's outfits on my bulletin board would upset the design of my room." Sarah's voice rose in indignation as she warmed to her subject. They both looked over at the bulletin board in question, which hung on the wall above Sarah's sewing machine. Almost every inch of the board's surface was covered with pictures of clothes carefully clipped from the pages of *Seventeen*, *Sassy*, *Teen*, and *IN Fashion*. Sarah intended to be a fashion designer, and she was starting her research as soon as possible.

"I kind of like Nicole's style," argued Micki, who today was dressed in cinnamon-colored cords that almost matched her short red hair, and a long-sleeved khaki-and-white-striped polo jersey. "Not everyone has your flair for creating trends, remember."

"Nicole doesn't, that's for sure!" Sarah retorted. She chuckled. "Little Miss Prim-and-Proper! I wish a tornado would — "

"A tornado would what?" Micki prompted as Sarah sat in sudden silence, one hand clapped over her mouth. "Hey, are you okay?"

Sarah nodded, dropping her hand. Micki Davis might be the only person besides her

Aunt Pam who knew anything about her deepest secret, but even Micki wouldn't believe what Sarah could actually do if she concentrated hard enough on her wishes.

As if reading the other girl's thoughts, Micki asked, "Sarah, you wouldn't actually cast a spell on your own sister, would you? I thought you said you weren't that kind of — well, you know."

"Witch." Sarah let the word hang between them for a moment. "There's nothing wrong with saying it, you know. And I'm not that kind of witch. If there's a way to do awful things, my, um, my trainer wouldn't let me find out how to do them."

After the chaos she'd created while trying out the powers she'd "inherited" when she turned thirteen, Sarah had shared her secret with Micki, including the fact that her Aunt Pam was a witch as well and was her teacher. Sarah had been relieved to have her best friend as a confidante, *especially* after she had made Waterview High disappear.

"Do something for now!" Micki begged. "I love when you make magic."

"Just a little thing," Sarah agreed hesitantly. "I'm not going to use my powers frivolously anymore. I promised Aunt Pam I wouldn't."

But for Micki's sake, she stared at her dresser until the drawers started moving in and out as if on their own accord.

"That's so neat!" Micki said enthusiastically. "You're better than David Copperfield, Sarah. Of course, he does it all with just tricks."

"Mmm." Sarah nodded, relieved Micki thought her powers were exciting and not scary.

"So," Micki went on, "were you really considering putting some spell on Nicole?"

"Of course not! It's just that. . . . Well, let's say I like to be careful what I wish for."

"Just in case, you mean?" Micki said. "In case you might wish for something and get more than you bargained for? Like the high school disappearing?"

"That's right. Just in case," Sarah agreed eagerly. She wondered what Micki would say if she told her about the time she'd wished stuffy old Jonathan Brooks would like Micki. She nearly groaned aloud remembering the results of that dreadful experience. Jonathan and Micki had become totally besotted with one another, and Micki had turned into a bad joke of a super-preppie, talking as if she had lockjaw and preferring foreign films set in countries where it always rained, to the classic horror films she and Sarah had always adored.

"I guess being a witch is more complicated than I thought," Micki remarked.

"You can say that again! Hey, how about calling Matt and seeing if he wants to watch the original *Dracula*?" she asked, eager to shift the subject away from discussing herself. "It's on *Sunday Supernatural Theater* at six o'clock."

"Good idea." Micki leaned over the edge of the bed to pick up the phone, which had been moved to the floor to make room on Sarah's bedside table for assorted pattern catalogues and the latest fashion magazines.

With his unruly sandy hair and eyeglasses, Matt Neville looked like the original whiz kid, and, in fact, both Sarah and Micki agreed Matt was the smartest person they'd ever known; real genius material. But Matt wasn't the kind of guy to lord it over anyone else just because he'd been getting straight A's since the first grade, and he wasn't king of the nerds, either. He was funny and wonderful, and he'd been Sarah and Micki's close friend for what seemed like forever.

"Matt says we should come watch the movie at his house," Micki announced after she'd hung up. "Not only do the Nevilles have that big wide-screen TV, but his mother just stocked the freezer with half-gallons of blueberry cheesecake ice cream."

"I knew he'd be up for *Dracula*. He's the only person who appreciates horror movies the way we do."

"Yeah." Micki chuckled. "Remember back in third or fourth grade when he decided he wanted to change his name to Mothra? Remember what his mother said?"

Shaking her head in amusement, Sarah lifted Bandit off her lap. The cat gave a plaintive mew of discontent.

"They say pets are like their owners," Micki said, as she stood and slipped back into her penny loafers. "Maybe Bandit's mad about missing a good horror flick."

"No, he just hates having a good lap pulled out from under him." Sarah looked at her pet, who'd curled up atop her pillow and was in the process of giving himself a grooming.

"Actually, I guess you and Bandit aren't alike at all," Micki admitted. "After all, cats are known to be fastidious creatures, aren't they? And everyone knows that 'neatness' is not your middle name."

"Cute," Sarah said dryly as they left the room. "Very cute. Maybe you should go down to the Improv in Hollywood and try to get a job writing for stand-up comics. Just the new comics, of course."

"Why just the new ones?"

"Because," Sarah was grinning now, "the older ones have been around long enough to learn what's really funny!"

"I don't care how long ago that movie was made, it's still scary!" Micki insisted a few hours later as the closing credits for *Dracula* rolled across the TV screen in the Neville's pine-paneled family room.

"It gives me the creeps every time I see it," Matt admitted. "I'd even wear cloves of garlic around my neck to school tomorrow — except that I'd hate to be accused of smelling worse than the food in the cafeteria!"

"Speaking of school. . . ." Yawning, Sarah pulled herself up from the deep cushions of the couch. "I've still got twenty pages of history to read tonight. And I'm willing to bet Ms. Hines is going to call on me in class tomorrow." The history teacher had made a point of singling Sarah out ever since the day Sarah had given in to temptation and used her powers to visualize her history text during an exam, only to discover she'd had no choice but to repeat the passages aloud word for word. Now Ms. Hines went out of her way to make sure Sarah was actually learning the material covered and not just memorizing it. "And I'm so bored with the Civil War!"

"But the War Between the States was one of the most important conflicts in our nation's history!" Matt insisted. "The Blue and the Gray. . . Brother against brother. . . Abe Lincoln. . . Robert E. Lee. . . Ulysses S. Grant." His thin face gleamed with awe and excitement. "It was anything but boring."

"Give me Scarlett O'Hara any day," Sarah said.

Both Micki and Matt stared. "Um, I don't know how to tell you this, Sarah," Micki finally said, her voice rich with sarcasm, "but not only was Scarlett O'Hara *not* an important figure in the Civil War, she wasn't even real. She was a character, as in fictional character, remember?"

"I *know* that," Sarah said.

"Come to think of it, I don't recall seeing *Gone With the Wind* on the history shelves at the library," Matt chimed in impishly. "It's all a bunch of romantic claptrap."

"Romantic claptrap?" Sarah gasped in feigned horror. "Why, Ah do declare, Mistuh

Neville, I lak a man with a l'il mo' romance in his heart."

"And marbles in his head?" Matt snickered.

"I *liked* studying about the Confederacy," Sarah insisted stubbornly. "And I'll bet there were lots of belles just like Scarlett, and men like Rhett Butler and Ashley Wilkes. But now that we're studying the war itself. . . . All those battles, battles, battles! How's a person supposed to remember all those places and dates?" She slathered the accent on thick again and did the best she could at batting her eyelids. "Why, it's all Ah can do to keep track of the names on mah dance card!"

The others joined in her laughter. "You'd have made some match for Scarlett O'Hara, Sarah," Micki said.

"Not after that blueberry cheesecake ice cream," Sarah groaned. "Scarlett O'Hara had the tiniest waist in three counties, didn't she?"

"Well, as Scarlett herself said, 'tomorrow is another day!' And I'd better go home and get ready for it," Micki said.

"You know, I just realized something pretty historic," Matt said as he saw the girls to the door. "The school's Tasty Meat Loaf probably dates back to Civil War days. Isn't that amazing?"

"How do you know that?" Micki and Sarah asked in unison.

"Simple. Even today its colors are still those of the North and the South — blue and gray!"

"Gross!"

"You're disgusting, Matt Neville!"

And, arm in arm, the two girls headed down the street.

Chapter 2

"A very interesting thing about the artichoke, kids," Sarah heard her father enthusiastically explaining to Simon and Nicole as she approached the dining room the next morning. "It's not actually a vegetable at all. It's an herb."

"Gee, you could have fooled me, Dad," seventeen-year-old Simon was saying as Sarah entered the room. His head, blond like his father's, was bent over his plate as he studied the mass congealing there. "I find it hard to believe the artichoke's even considered a food!"

Uh-oh, Sarah thought, Dad's been experimenting with recipes again! But before she could slip out of the room, she was spotted.

"Ah, just in time!" Dr. David Connell had spied his youngest child. "You can get the last of the frittata while it's hot! Your mother had to leave early, so she missed these."

"Frittata?" Sitting, Sarah poured herself a glass of orange juice from the pitcher on the table, trying not to look at the serving platter standing alongside the juice. "Maybe just a taste," she agreed reluctantly, unwilling to hurt her father when he labored so over his gourmet concoctions. "What exactly *is* frittata?"

"Oh, it's very interesting, Sarah," Nicole crooned teasingly. "Why not just take all that's left and see for yourself?" The mischievous sparkle in her eyes showed that Nicole had clearly recovered from her snit of the day before.

Resignedly, Sarah spooned some of the glop onto her plate. By now, all three Connell children had learned to live with their father's cookery, if not to enjoy it.

"Mmm," Sarah murmured wanly after managing to choke down a mouthful of the dry mass, "it *is* interesting. What did you say it is, Dad?"

"I didn't say, but it's kind of an Italian omelette. Just a blend of eggs, artichoke hearts, basil, and garlic."

"Garlic!" Nicole quickly raised a hand and

blew onto it, testing her own breath. "I can't go to school reeking of garlic!"

"It's just a pinch, dear, not the whole clove. Come on, clean your plates! It's good to start the day with a nourishing breakfast, you know. Speaking of which" — he pushed back his chair and got to his feet, inclining his head toward the wing of the house that had been converted to his medical offices — "I've got Mrs. Petersen coming in for nutritional counseling any minute. She feeds her two-year-old sugared cereals and brownies for breakfast. Would you believe it?"

"Thank goodness for the garbage disposal," Sarah muttered under her breath as her father left the room.

"You mean you aren't going to eat all that?" Nicole asked in mock surprise. "And here I was willing to let you have the rest of mine, too!"

Simon picked up his plate and headed for the kitchen. "After I dump this, I think I'll bike around the block a few times. See if I can head off Mrs. Petersen's kid and bribe him into giving up one of those brownies."

"Sarah, if you clear off the table while I run upstairs and grab my jacket and books, you can hitch a ride to school. LeeAnn's coming to pick me up," Nicole said.

"I can't wait till my friends have cars," Sarah confessed. "A ride would be great. Then I'll have time to skim my history reading just one more time."

After Nicole left the room, Sarah carried the dirty dishes out to the kitchen. Then, even though she'd promised herself — and her Aunt Pam — not to use her powers lightly anymore, she closed her eyes and concentrated hard, whispering under her breath, "Dishes, be washed and put away."

When Sarah opened her eyes, there wasn't a dirty plate, pot, or pan to be seen. If only I could do that with history class, she thought. But her history book was waiting for her, so, grabbing it along with the antique baseball jacket she'd brought downstairs to wear over her denim minidress, Sarah hurried off to meet Nicole.

"Hey, you did well in history class this morning, Sarah. I never would have guessed you were an expert on the Battle of Antietam." Tina Jordan's deep brown eyes sparkled as she deposited her lunch tray on the cafeteria table and sat down to join Sarah, Micki, and Heather Larson.

"I'm an expert on all the Civil War battles," Sarah said airily. "Only I can't remember more than one at a time. Since our reading covered only Antietam, I was in luck. If Fort Sumter or Appomattox had been thrown in, I'd have been in water so hot it'd be boiling!"

"Sarah, look! David Shaw is over there. You're still going out with him, aren't you?" Tina asked. "I think he's terrific."

"I do, too," Sarah said enthusiastically, looking at David, with his green eyes and coal-black hair. Sarah would never forget how excited she'd been that first time he'd asked her out. "We don't see a whole lot of each other because he's so busy with his job at the Pizza Palace, not to mention JV sports and homework. It's just as well, actually, since keeping up in history and French are practically full-time jobs for *me* this year."

Micki groaned. "Ditto French for me. How can a language sound so pretty and be so hard to learn?"

"It's no harder than English," Matt informed her. "Imagine trying to learn English as a second language. All those words that look alike and sound different — like 'tough' and 'through' and 'bough.' "

"And the verbs!" Heather put in. " 'I am,' 'you are,' 'she is,' 'I was,' 'you were,' 'we have been.' It's impossible!"

Allison Rogers walked by at just that moment. "There, there, Heather," she said mockingly. "You've got three more years to learn basic grammar before you graduate. I know it isn't easy for *some* people."

"How can anyone get their kicks from being just plain nasty?" Tina asked in disgust as Allison moved on.

"It keeps Allison cooled out till she can get home and tear the wings off some flies," Matt answered.

"Gross!" Micki pushed back her tray. "Glad I'm finished eating. Sarah, you want to head up toward French class?"

"Sure." Sarah stood, patting her flat tummy. "Too much ice cream last night, too much pasta today. How will Ah ever get a seventeen-inch-waist lak Scarlett?"

"Seventeen inches?" Tina snorted. "Forget it, girl! I wear a size six, and I don't think I've had a seventeen-inch waist since I was in a playpen!"

"I wonder how they stayed so slim during the Civil War," Heather mused aloud. "Eating all those grits and flapjacks!"

"It was probably the Tasty Meat Loaf," Matt put in.

As the two girls left the cafeteria, Micki murmured, "I don't suppose it would be possible for you to use a little mumbo-jumbo to help me remember my French verb conjugations?"

"Sorry," Sarah said, genuinely regretful. "It doesn't work that way. Besides, I'm trying to lay off using my powers frivolously, remember?"

"There's nothing frivolous about French class," Micki muttered. "Or about the way my mom's going to ground me if I don't get a high grade on the next French test."

"I know. That's how I feel about history. But there's really nothing to do but study. Sometimes I don't think progress is all that hot, you know? Sometimes I wouldn't mind going back to those days when girls studied embroidery and painting and poetry. It sure beats battles and verbs."

"You don't mean that, do you?" Micki's voice was shocked.

"No," Sarah assured her friend, but as they continued down the hall, she pictured herself in a fine muslin gown sitting on the wide veranda of an old plantation house, sipping fresh-made lemonade and basting lace onto a crisp taffeta petticoat. And it didn't strike her as a half-bad way to pass an afternoon. But French verbs — that was different. *C'est la vie, Sarah*, she told herself as she took her seat in the classroom, *C'est la* gnarly *vie!*

Chapter 3

"What's wrong, Sarah?" Pamela Huntley asked her niece as she steered her little car away from the mall where the Pizza Palace was located. "Didn't you like your dinner?"

"Dinner was fine. What's not to like about a pepperoni-and-mushroom deep-dish pizza?" In her own ears, Sarah's voice sounded dead and listless.

"I liked David," her aunt went on cheerfully. "He seems genuinely nice. And what a doll! He reminds me of a younger Rob Lowe."

Sarah was silent until her aunt had pulled to a stop in front of Plates and Pages, the combination tea shop–bookstore, which was also Aunt Pam's house. "Why not come in and have a cup of tea? We haven't had much of a chance to talk lately."

"Sure," Sarah replied with a shrug.

It wasn't until Sarah was comfortably settled, a cup of hibiscus tea in her hand and Grumble the Siamese cat in her lap, that Pamela Huntley suggested gently, "Why not tell me what's bugging you, Sarah? You've been down in the dumps all night — not to mention that you haven't looked at me once without glaring. Is it something I've done?"

Sarah shook her head. "Not really."

"Is it David?"

"Sort of."

"What's got you so ticked off then?"

Sarah exhaled loudly. "Everything, I guess. I mean, what's the big deal about being a witch when I can't do anything meaningful with my powers? It's all a big ripoff!"

"What were you thinking of doing?" Pam asked innocently. "Making the high school disappear again?"

"Of course not! You know I'd never do that!" Sarah protested. "But putting books on shelves and washing dishes? I mean, big deal! Is that all my powers mean — another labor-saving device, like a dishwasher?"

"Ah, now I see," her Aunt Pam said softly. She paused to take a sip of her tea, then continued, her voice even, "This all started when David told you he'd have to work this whole weekend and the next, didn't it?"

Sarah stared at her challengingly. "Why wouldn't you let me do something to change it? To get David a weekend off?"

"Do it if you really want, Sarah. I can't stop you. All I'm trying to do is teach you to use your powers sensibly — and unselfishly. For instance, why do you think David works at the Pizza Palace? Because it's so much fun?"

"Of course not. He works because he needs the money."

"And you were going to deprive him of that money just so he could take you to the movies?"

Sarah tilted her head. "I didn't think of it that way."

"What you said to me was, 'I think I'll concentrate real hard and wish David didn't have to work next weekend.' Didn't it occur to you that he could ask for the weekend off if he didn't need the money?"

"What if I'd done it in a way so David still got paid?"

"How? How could you have done that without hurting someone, either David or his boss or somebody else?"

"I guess you're right," Sarah admitted reluctantly. "But then why be a witch at all? It's not so great."

Her aunt laughed. "For one thing, you don't choose to be a witch, Sarah. You know that! If you're a witch, you're a witch. And those powers are yours whether you want them or not. What's important is to learn to use them for good. Not to use them for personal gain or to hurt other people or as mischievous tricks to get rid of boredom."

"I didn't do any of those things on purpose!" Sarah exclaimed, knowing her mother's younger sister was referring to the times when Sarah's powers had gone wrong. "Well, not most of them, anyway."

"And that's why young witches always have someone like myself in their lives — to gradually teach them to use the full range of their powers in the right way."

"But can't I have any fun with them?" Sarah protested. "You make witches sound like dreary do-gooders!"

"Oh, you'll have fun, all right!" Aunt Pam promised. "Just you wait and see all the exciting things you'll be able to do one day. But you can't be so impatient, Sarah," she cautioned. "You've inherited a great deal of very powerful magic, and you've got to use it with care."

"It's not as if I'm a baby, you know," Sarah argued.

"Of course you're not!" Aunt Pam's golden eyes sparkled, and her black hair gleamed in the lamplight as she leaned over to squeeze her niece's hand. "But imagine that you'd never seen matches or fire before. If I handed you a pack of matches and left the room, you could cause a lot of damage through your own innocence of fire, couldn't you?"

Slowly, Sarah nodded. "All right, I see your point. But. . . . Oh, Aunt Pam! Schoolwork is so awful this year, and now David and I can't even go out on weekends to make up for it! I'm bored and cranky all the time, and it doesn't seem fair that I can't use my magic to feel better!"

"Special powers aren't given to people as a pick-me-up, Sarah. I guess what I mean is that even witches get down in the dumps sometimes. I know I do."

"You do?" Sarah asked, marveling that someone like her aunt, who always seemed so on top of everything, could have bad days.

"Of course I do, silly!" Aunt Pam laughed.

Sarah smiled. "How can you put up with me when I'm such a pain, Aunt Pam?"

"It's easy," Aunt Pam said warmly. "You remind me so much of myself when I was your age. Now, just to cheer you up even more, I'm going to teach you something new, and it's something that should keep boredom away, too!"

Sarah went home in a drastically improved mood from the sulk she'd been in upon arriving at her aunt's. The "something new" Aunt Pam taught her was terrific. "It's like having your own mental VCR," she'd said enthusiastically after learning how to actually "see" any movie she wanted right in her own room.

"All you have to do is wish for the movie to appear on your wall, and you can watch whatever you like," Aunt Pam promised.

"And nobody else can see or hear it?"

"That's right," her aunt told her. "From *The Wizard of Oz* to *Big*, you can have a private screening whenever you want."

"How could I have thought being a witch wasn't a big deal?" Sarah asked when her Aunt Pam dropped her off at home. "Think of all the money I'll save on movies!"

As she pushed open the front door to the house, she was sure she'd never be bored again.

* * *

"Want to go see that new movie playing at the Elgin?" Micki asked when Sarah called the following Saturday morning. "Tina and I are going to the two o'clock show."

Without stopping to think, Sarah said, "Oh, it's not very good."

"How do you know? It just opened yesterday."

Sarah didn't want to admit she'd already screened every new movie in town in the privacy of her room. "Oh, I heard it got mixed reviews," she said lamely.

"Look, do you want to see it or not?" Micki asked.

"I guess not," Sarah admitted. "Besides, I should really study for the history quiz next week."

"But all you've been doing lately is studying!" Micki protested.

"There's no such thing as too much studying," Sarah said brightly. "Anyhow, I've got to get a decent grade on that exam, and it covers every single battle we've studied this term. All those dates!"

"Tina and I were thinking of going roller-skating later on. Are you up for that? Or too busy studying?"

"No, I'd love to go," Sarah said quickly, knowing she'd been neglecting Micki in favor of her own magic movies. "And you and Tina can tell me all about the movie."

She hung up the phone, regretting now that she'd greedily conjured up every new film in town. When she should have been studying, no less! Sighing, Sarah opened her history notebook. "What two important events happened in 1861, Bandit?" she asked her indifferent cat. "Very good! Abraham Lincoln was inaugurated, and the Confederate Army occupied Fort Sumter."

She meant well, she really did. But by the time Micki called to make arrangements to meet at Skating World, Sarah had committed very few dates to memory. Instead, she'd watched *Gone With the Wind* on her bedroom wall.

In spite of the fact that she rescreened the story of Tara and Scarlett O'Hara three more times before Tuesday arrived, Sarah walked into history class feeling confident the day of the test. It hadn't hurt that Kirk Tanner had stopped at her locker that morning.

"Nice threads, Connell!" he'd said, eyeing

her appreciatively. "You're a shoe-in for best-dressed your senior year."

"You think so?" She'd blushed with pleasure. She'd worn her very favorite new outfit — black tights, a black turtleneck and a black and white polka-dot flounced skirt she'd made herself — in the hopes it would bring her luck on her history test. Now it was already bringing her good fortune in unexpected places.

"Definitely," he assured her. "Seriously, Sarah, how about contributing a fashion column to the *Sentinel*? We could use your creativity."

"Do you mean that, Kirk?" she'd asked, her heart pounding so loudly she was afraid he might hear it.

He'd nodded, saying, "Let's get together later in the week to talk about it. After school one day, maybe."

She still felt aglow at the thought of writing a column as she took her seat in Ms. Hines's classroom. She did wish she'd opted for watching *Gone With the Wind* one less time and studying harder instead. But she was pretty sure she had a handle on all those dates. They flashed through her mind as the rest of the class staggered in, some grumbling under their breath at the prospect of what was to come.

"Good luck, Sarah," Micki whispered as she passed.

"You, too," Sarah answered aloud, while silently, she was reviewing, *1862, Jefferson Davis becomes president of the Confederate States; 1865, Union forces take back Fort Sumter.*

Sarah was fine until Ms. Hines announced, "Today's test will consist of two essay questions. First, tell which Civil War battles you consider to have been the most important and give reasons for your choices. Second, discuss weaknesses in the Confederacy, beginning before the Civil War, which led to the South's defeat."

Oh, no, Sarah thought. Not essay questions after I got all those dates down pat!

She decided to start with the second question first, since she had the best shot at getting some points for that one.

The Confederacy, she wrote, *was doomed by the time war was declared, because the Southerners underestimated the edge the North gained through industrialization.* She scribbled on, knowing she'd have to leave plenty of time to bluff her way through the first question, knowing only that she'd choose battles for which she had the dates at hand.

. . . and others believe the South could easily have taken steps to better prepare itself for the coming war, she continued, glancing at her watch. She'd give herself just four more minutes to finish with this part of the test. *But the Southerners, especially the plantation owners, wanted to eat, drink, and be merry. They lived for balls and cotillions, not bullets and cannons. . . ."*

Her mind drifted. Who wouldn't choose dancing and flirting over fighting and feuding? She wished she'd been around then to wear beautiful gowns with wide hoop skirts. She could have rivalled Scarlett O'Hara in high spirits and elegant taste, she was sure. And the men back then! Boys no older than David, wearing those impressive gray uniforms with boots.

Instead I have to be stuck in this stuffy room taking this stupid test, she thought resentfully. *Oh, how I wish I weren't here! I wish I could go back to those days before the Civil War, to living for balls and cotillions! Of course, Micki would be there, too, and a dreamy guy would be somewhere in the picture, somebody just like David. . . .*

A strange sleepiness overcame Sarah then, and she dropped her pencil onto the desk in front of her, her essay test forgotten.

Chapter 4

Even though the morning sunlight had slipped into her bedroom, Sarah snuggled more deeply into her pillow. Just a few more minutes, she told herself, and then I'll get up. She felt so sleepy and relaxed just lying there, she hated to move.

She rolled over onto her back, yawned, and opened her eyes. The white canopy above her was like a movie screen, she decided, upon which she might play back any dream she liked. She chuckled softly at her fanciful thinking. Of course the canopy wasn't a movie screen, it —

"A canopy!" Gasping the words aloud, she sprang to a sitting position. "But my bed doesn't *have* a canopy!"

Her heart pounded as her eyes traveled around the room. There was an old-fashioned washstand with a pitcher and bowl on it, a big wardrobe carved out of dark, gleaming wood, a fireplace — Where in the world was she, and how had she gotten there?

"What if I've been kidnapped?" she whispered. Oh, her poor parents! But, no, she told herself, of course she hadn't been kidnapped. This room was pretty fancy even if it was old-fashioned. Surely kidnappers didn't stash their victims in quaint Victorian guest houses.

Obviously, that was where she was, in a guest house done up with antiques, like the one where she and Aunt Pam had spent the night when they had driven up the coast to Big Sur. But why couldn't she remember arriving?

Don't panic, she told herself. Maybe you tripped and hit your head and you've got a touch of amnesia. Just think back. . . .

What had happened yesterday? she thought. She closed her eyes and tried to remember, but all that came into her mind was a picture of herself sitting in history class! She didn't remember eating lunch or leaving school or going home or *anything*.

"Uh-oh," she murmured, sinking back against the headboard. "Something weird's going on."

Just then she heard the sound of a latch opening. Looking toward the door, she watched — half terrified and half curious — as it swung open to reveal a big black woman wearing a long dress that looked as if it had been stitched together out of flour sacks, and a gingham apron. Around the woman's head was a scarf of the same material as her apron, but it wasn't worn kerchief-style, just wrapped and knotted in front. In her arms, the woman carried a big tray, from which wafted a heavenly aroma.

"Here's your breakfast, Miss Abigail," the woman announced as she crossed the room. She set the tray on a small table next to the bed. "Hot tea, ham and eggs, and biscuits fresh from the oven!"

"Miss *Who*? And who are *you*?"

"You still half asleep, Missy? It's me, Miss Abigail — Bertie, remember? I only raised you since you was a babe in arms is all I done!" she said, laughing. "So stop your staring and rub the sleep out of your eyes and eat this food while it's hot. Your mama wants you and your cousin Delphinea downstairs and dressed to go to town in an hour. She gave orders for Joseph to hitch up the horses. You eat, and I'll bring you some water to wash up with."

All Sarah could do was nod, afraid to trust her voice. I hope what I think may have happened didn't, she worried, slipping from the bed as soon as Bertie had left the room. She saw that she was wearing a long white cotton nightgown, its sleeves edged with lace. "Nice," she murmured, her fashion-consciousness intact in spite of her uneasiness. You didn't see much real handmade lace nowadays.

Nowadays. Sarah crept to the window and pulled back the drapes only to find herself staring down at white-dotted fields that stretched as far as the eye could see. And here and there, in uneven rows throughout the fields, she could see bent backs and black hands plucking their way through the greenery. "Cotton," she murmured. "They're picking cotton. I don't believe this!"

Hearing the door opening again behind her, she said, hoping she sounded casual, "You can just leave the water at the door, Bertie. I'll get it."

"Well, I see you've made yourself right at home!"

Beneath the molasses-like drawl, that angry voice was familiar. "Micki!" Sarah exclaimed as she wheeled around. "Are you a sight for sore eyes!"

Micki's face was scrunched together, as if part of it wanted to holler while the other part

35

wanted to cry. "Soon your eyes aren't going to be the only thing that's hurting you, Abigail Mannering! By the time I get through with you, you'll hurt all over!"

"Hold on!" Sarah threw out her arms, holding Micki off. She'd never seen her friend in such a state. "It's me, Sarah, Micki! Who's this Abigail Mannering, anyhow?"

"Don't play games with me, Sarah!" Micki's voice trembled. "This is scary, and it's all your fault. I just know it is!"

"Let's try to stay calm, Micki," Sarah said softly, slipping an arm around her friend's shoulders and leading her over to the bed. "I'm as mixed up and scared as you are. Are we where I think we are?"

"If you think we're down in Dixie before the Civil War, then we're exactly where you think we are," Micki retorted sharply, sounding a bit more like her old self — in spirit, at least.

"So who's Abigail Mannering? And how come you're talking like that?"

"*You're* Abigail Mannering now, just like I'm your cousin Delphinea Norcross! It's bad enough you got me into this, but I've got to be related to you, too," Micki moaned. "And Ah'm not talking any funnier than you."

Sarah strained her ears to hear herself as

she said, "I don't talk funny, but you sure do." What she heard was, "Ah doan talk funny, but y'all do."

"Hear it?"

Sarah nodded ruefully. "Now I know why I couldn't remember anything after history class. There wasn't any 'after history class,' was there? I sat there wishing we could be back in the days of the Old South together, and here we are."

"Yeah, here we are, all right," Micki said, her usual wryness coming back into her new voice, "not only in the Old South — but on the losing side!"

"Oh, deah!" Sarah couldn't help chuckling at her own lazy voice. "What have Ah done this time?"

"Whatever it was that you did, undo it, quick!"

"Let's not rush into anything, Micki," Sarah cautioned. She picked up a biscuit and took a big bite. "Did you eat?"

"A little bit," Micki admitted. "Only 'cause Daisy was standing there, and I didn't want her to think anything was funny, you know?"

"Who's Daisy?" Sarah asked, attacking her ham and eggs.

"Far as I could gather, she's Bertie's daughter. Her dad's name is Homer, and he oversees the slaves in the fields."

"Slaves! Oh, *no*! They are slaves, aren't they? Do you think I should tell Bertie they'll all soon be free?"

"Puh-leeze!" Micki eyes widened in panic. "Don't go telling Bertie anything! Or anybody else, for that matter. They'll think you're crazy. Or worse. Remember, Sarah, it's the 1800s. If you start telling people you're a witch from the twentieth century, we could both end up being burned at the stake! Let's just get out of here, okay?"

"First tell me how you learned all this stuff about Abigail and Delphinea."

Micki shrugged, helping herself to a biscuit. "Some of it I managed to get out of Daisy. The rest I just kind of *know*. I mean, it just sort of came to me when I was talking to Daisy. You probably know more about Abigail and Delphinea than you realize, Sarah."

"You think so?" Sarah asked doubtfully.

"Sure. Let's see. . . . Tell me about Abigail's brother Sam."

"Mah brother Sam?" Sarah said slowly. "Why, he's one of the most sought-after bachelors in all of Georgia, although I wouldn't be surprised if he asks Marybeth Mayhew to be his bride one of these days. Of course, Sam isn't here now. He's with the Confederate Forces in Montgomery, and he's rarin' to go into battle with those awful Yankees."

Sarah stopped suddenly, her eyes wide. "Now how did I know all that?"

Micki nodded wisely. "See what I mean? That's how I knew I was here visiting my aunt and uncle and Cousin Abigail and that I'd come from Birmingham. And that we're both seventeen years old."

"Seventeen!" Sarah gasped. "Micki, how can we be older than we were in Waterview?"

"Beats me. It sure is spooky, though. So how's about you just witchy-wish us out of here the same as you witchy-wished us in?"

"I didn't mean to do it, Micki. Honest! I was just sitting there thinking how romantic everything was back in those days — um, *these* days. And I thought how neat it would have been to have been around in the days of Scarlett O'Hara and the Confederacy and. . . ."

"And here we are," Micki finished for her. "That's swell. And it's been a real unforgettable experience, Sarah. Now, how about getting us out of here? Right away?"

Sarah stared out the window, blinking so Micki couldn't see she was about to cry out of fear and frustration. Sighing, she shook her head. "I can't, Micki," she said in a tiny voice. "I'm afraid to."

"How come? Since when have you scared so easily?"

"It's not as if I ever did anything like this before, Micki!" Sarah said sharply, her usual spirited manner returning. "I'm not a genie, you know. And I don't want to get us in any worse trouble."

"What could be worse?" Micki asked, sounding just curious now and not so angry.

"It's hard to explain, but I shouldn't have been able to do this at all. See, I'm just an apprentice witch, not a full-fledged witch. But even full-fledged witches don't have the ability to time travel at the drop of a hat. So I don't know how I did it. I mean, there we were in class, and now here we are with the Civil War about to break out all around us! This isn't a dream! Abigail and Delphinea were real people. So where are they now that we're them? And what happened to those girls in Waterview — Sarah and Micki — when we came here?"

Micki's voice was hushed with surprise as she asked, "You mean we might have just *disappeared* in the middle of history class?"

Sarah shrugged. "Beats me. But I'm afraid to try to get us back there right away, Micki. I mean, what if I goof and we go the wrong way? We could end up back with the Neanderthals! I just don't know how to get us out of here and guarantee we get back to where we started from!"

"Don't do a thing, Sarah," Micki said quickly. "Prehistoric times — can you imagine? Not that being stuck here is any better. We've got to figure something out! I can't stay stuck in a world without jogging shoes or VCRs or women's rights!"

"Or rock 'n' roll or shopping malls!" Sarah chimed in. Then she smiled slightly. "Or history tests or Nicole bugging me or my father's cooking. Say, we may be better off than we think!"

Micki chuckled, but then her face turned serious again. "It's not funny, Sarah. You've *got* to do something!"

"I've got it!" Sarah snapped her fingers.

"You've figured out how to get us out of here?" Micki asked hopefully.

Sarah nodded. "I'm sure that if I concentrate really hard I should be able to communicate with Aunt Pam. She'll tell me how to get us out of here! She can do anything."

"Go for it then!" Micki encouraged her.

"Okay. Now, don't say a word, because I need perfect quiet." Sarah closed her eyes so tight they hurt as she concentrated on her Aunt Pam, picturing in her mind her aunt's calm, pretty face, golden eyes, and long, black hair. *Help me, Aunt Pam, she said silently. Help me this one more time and I promise I'll never wish for anything foolish again. Just let me open my eyes and find myself back in history class or in my room at home. Get me and Micki out of here, please! We're scared and we want to go home.*

Sarah was only barely aware of her own breathing — she was concentrating so hard on her mental picture of Aunt Pam, waiting for the image to speak to her, to tell her what to do next. Then the image started to fade as Sarah felt something warm, furry, and alive brushing against her bare ankle. "Bandit!" she thought happily, knowing she was safe and sound back in her own bedroom with her cat demanding a cuddle.

Her eyes still closed, Sarah reached down and picked up the cat, holding it suspended in front of her so the first thing she'd see was her little black cat's adorable face.

But the furry face that met her own was

ginger, with eyes the color of maple syrup. "You're not Bandit!" she groaned. She jerked around to see Micki, still seated next to her on the canopied bed. "And we're not home!"

"The cat's name is Clementine," Micki said somberly. "And yours is Abigail, and mine is Delphinea. And we're stuck here in the awful, old nineteenth century!" She got to her feet. "This is a nightmare, Sarah, a true nightmare."

"I'll get us out of this, Micki. I promise I will!" Sarah vowed.

"I hope so," Mick said grimly. "Because you know something? Compared to what's happening to us right now, *Dracula* wasn't a horror story at all. It was a comedy. A thigh-slapping, side-splitting, rib-tickling comedy!" And with that, Micki stormed out, stopping at the door just long enough to say, in a drawl that dripped honey and venom, "And now you all had best shake a leg, gal. Your mama'll be waiting for us. We all are goin' to town, 'member?"

Sarah buried her face in the cat's luxuriant fur. "Oh, Clementine," she muttered, "I really did it this time, didn't I?"

Chapter 5

"Thank goodness, it fits!" Sarah muttered feverishly, after she had finally managed to cram one foot into a narrow black leather lace-up boot. She tried putting her weight on it. "Ouch!" The darned thing pinched like crazy on a foot accustomed to sneakers. She tugged the other boot on, then stood admiring herself in the long cheval glass.

"You make a pretty picture in your undies, Abigail Mannering," she said aloud to the reflection that greeted her. It was odd, because she could actually make out the features of the real Abigail underneath her own. It was as if Sarah's own face had been drawn on tracing paper and then placed over the other's. Of course, no one else except Micki could see Sarah Connell there.

She made a romantic study, she thought, in her black cotton stockings and lace and beribboned petticoat and camisole. "Now, which dress would Abigail wear to go to town?" she wondered as she opened the heavy doors of the carved wooden wardrobe. Maybe the report she'd done on historical fashion would help her now.

A knock at the door startled her, then she heard Bertie call, "Are you ready for me to lace you up, Miss Abigail?"

Lace her up? Stupidly, Sarah stared down at her boots. Wasn't she supposed to have laced them up herself? "Uh, come on in, Bertie. I'm almost ready to go," she answered, hoping Bertie could help her choose just the right dress so she wouldn't have to.

"Why, you aren't ready to be laced!" Bertie sniffed in exasperation when she saw Sarah standing in her underclothes and boots. "Here, let me get your corset for you. You know how impatient your mama gets when she's kept waiting."

As she pulled what looked to Sarah like a collapsed lampshade from one of the bureau drawers, Bertie asked, "Which dress are you plannin' to wear to town? I've got to know how tight to lace you."

Sarah's stomach quivered as she recalled the scene where Scarlett clung for dear life to the bedposts as Mammy laced her body to fit into her tight-waisted dress. "I thought I'd wear something comfortable today, Bertie," she said. "Which do you think?" She nodded toward the open wardrobe.

"Which do I think?" Bertie sounded startled at being asked to choose. "Maybe the blue cotton you wore to tea at the Mayhews' last week?"

"That sounds fine," Sarah said gratefully. She took the corset Bertie handed her, staring at it blankly for a long moment. Now, which end went where? She wished she could remember just how they'd done it in the movie!

"You *are* in a fog this morning! Give it over, and take hold of the bedpost, Miss Abigail."

Sarah did as she was told, and Bertie's capable hands fitted the corset about her waist, laces to the back. As Sarah felt the sharp yank of the laces being pulled tight, she gasped, not just from the air being forced out of her lungs, but from the sharp sensation of the whalebone stays as they bit into her ribcage. She might get that seventeen-inch waist yet — if she didn't faint before Bertie was done lacing her up!

At long last, Bertie grunted. "There you are. Now, let me get your dress."

Sarah kept her grip on the bedpost, afraid to stand alone until the stars stopped dancing before her eyes. How could she possibly get through the rest of the day laced in so tightly? She couldn't even manage a full exhalation or inhalation, able only to draw tiny sips of air into her lungs before the stays refused to let her diaphragm move another millimeter. No wonder women always used to complain about having "the vapors," she thought. Why, that was no more than a quaint phrase for oxygen starvation!

"Here. You need your crinoline with the blue," Bertie said, approaching with what appeared to be about ten yards of stiff netting, the bottom edges of which were held out in every direction by a metal hoop. "Let me slip this over your head and tie it round the back. Then we'll get you into your dress."

Sarah did as she was told, trying not to show her amazement at the abundance of material with which her body was being loaded down.

Even after she'd assisted Bertie in slipping the deep blue cotton dress — which fell below her ankles — over her head, Sarah couldn't move. She had to stand still for what seemed like forever as Bertie fastened the twenty or so hooks that ran from her hips to the nape of her neck in back.

Still, rechecking her reflection after the dress was in place, Sarah had to admit that, discomfort or not, she liked the way the corset made her waistline look downright minuscule. And the blue dress was beautiful, with velvet ribbons of a paler hue cascading from flounces at her hips, and sleeves that puffed at the shoulders.

"It's perfect!" Sarah whispered.

"I always did like the way that dress fit you. You look mighty pretty."

"Oh, thank you, Bertie!" Sarah exclaimed. "I suppose I should hurry down to Mama before she's out of sorts with me."

"Let me get the rest of your things," Bertie told her, heading back to the wardrobe.

The rest of her things? Sarah was dumb-struck. How much more could a single person wear to go to town?

"Here," Bertie said. "Your gloves, your shawl, your bonnet, and your reticule." Sarah looked in amazement at the four items, the last of which reminded her of her mother's antique beaded evening bag. The bonnet, a blue straw with more velvet ribbons flowing, she put on her head; the gloves she put on her hands, and the shawl she threw lightly over her shoulders.

"Now, be off with you!" Bertie said good-naturedly. "And you be sure to enjoy your outing with Miss Delphinea."

"I'm sure I will, Bertie," Sarah said faintly, as she took her first hesitant steps, the shoes pinching, the stays poking, and the hoopskirt billowing out in every direction.

This was going to be a real experience, she realized as she gingerly made her way down the hallway to the wide, winding staircase she could spy at its end. The hoop kept her skirt splayed out a good foot in every direction, and it swayed and buckled with every step, making her feel as if she were steering the QE2 into port and not just herself down a hallway.

The stairs were even worse, since the hoop swayed her skirts up first in front and then in back with every step, while she felt weakened by the sheer abundance of the clothing she transported.

It's got to be ninety degrees in the shade, she thought miserably, feeling rivulets of perspiration trickle down the back of her neck. This was shorts and sandals weather, and here she was, wearing an ocean of undergarments, gloves, a bonnet, a long-sleeved gown, a taffeta shawl, and heavy cotton stockings! No wonder the South was going to lose the war!

At the foot of the stairs, she stopped to catch her breath as well as was possible under the circumstances. The Mannerings must have been rich, she decided. The entrance hall in which she stood had a floor of polished marble. Its walls of gleaming mahogany held massive oil paintings of what she assumed were generations of Mannerings, and through an archway, she could see what she supposed was the living room, or front parlor, which must have been thirty feet long and which overflowed with furniture. She spotted at least two velvet settees, numerous prickly-looking wingback chairs, and more bric-a-brac than was contained in the Waterview Museum.

Tottering to the double front doors, she pushed one open and was met with a scene so striking it took her breath away again. A circular drive came almost up to the wide veranda that ran from one end of the house all the way to the next. In the distance, she could see other buildings which she supposed were also part of the plantation. The rolling meadow that fell away from the house had its lush surface broken by fragrant camellias and leafy trees.

But the most imposing sight was the carriage! Of black laquered wood, its sides were open, while what must have been the forefather to the convertible's top, offered shade from the hot sun. Hitched in front of the box seat where the driver would sit were two huge chestnut horses. A stool had been drawn up next to the carriage, and an elderly black man stood next to it. Facing each other on the carriage's burgundy leather seats were a darkhaired woman Sarah assumed to be Abigail's mother and a laced, bonneted, very red-faced Micki Davis.

Seeing her daughter, Mrs. Mannering called impatiently, "Oh, Abigail, must you always keep others waiting! You're too vain by far, daughter!"

"Thank you, Joseph," Sarah said sweetly as the man gave her a hand up. Then, settling next to Micki, she said, "I'm genuinely sorry, Mama. Bertie had trouble lacing my stays."

"Perhaps because you insist upon having them laced so tightly, Abigail." Mrs. Mannering's lips were pursed, but her brilliant blue eyes were shining.

"I just long to be as lovely as you were at my age, Mama," Sarah said meekly, ignoring a soft snort from Micki.

"Ah, Abigail, you do resemble the Norcross

family more closely than the Mannerings!" the woman said with a proud laugh as Joseph snapped his whip at the horses and the carriage rocked into movement. "Charm and vanity go hand in hand. But you shall have to tame your headstrong ways one day. Preoccupation with one's self is all very well in a young girl, but it will never do once you become some gentleman's wife."

"Of course not, Mama," Sarah agreed, thinking that old Abigail Mannering had a lot in common with the twentieth century's Sarah Connell.

"You should strive to be more like your cousin Delphinea."

"Were you sharing memories of Birmingham while you waited for me, Delphinea?" Sarah asked impishly.

Micki's look shot daggers. "No, Cousin Abigail. I was simply remarking on what a pleasure it is every time I come to Meadowhaven." She sighed dramatically. "Such a beautiful place!"

"I'm sure Mama can never hear our home praised too much." Exciting conversations they had in those days, Sarah thought wryly, hoping the drive to town wouldn't last too long. She could feel the tenseness in Micki's body next to hers, and she wondered if her friend was as physically and mentally uncomfortable as she was. How could you make small talk with a woman you'd never met before when she was supposed to be your mother?

The carriage moved at a leisurely pace down dirt roads lined on either side by cotton fields. As it went by, the slaves working there stood to watch it pass and the men removed their hats. Sarah saw children in the fields, who couldn't have been much older than eight or nine, and her heart went out to them. But Micki was right — she'd best keep her mouth shut. She couldn't change the course of slavery, so she must take comfort in the knowledge that all these people would be freed in the near future.

"A penny for your thoughts, Abigail," Mrs. Mannering said. Sarah didn't even realize the comment was directed at her until Micki gave her a very modern poke in the ribs.

"Who, me?" she sputtered. "Oh, why, I was just thinking how nice it will be to spend some time in town." No sooner had she said it then she worried that she'd made a mistake. What if "town" was an absolute fleapit?

But Mrs. Mannering seemed satisfied with her answer, and Sarah relaxed again until she was asked, "Where do you girls want to go first?"

"Oh, wherever Delphinea wishes to go," Sarah said quickly. "After all, *she's* our guest."

"You're too sweet, Cousin Abigail," Micki said through clenched teeth. "But I suggest we follow your mama's wishes."

"Either Ballard's or Minton's will have the best selection."

"Perhaps we should visit both establishments," Sarah suggested, wondering, best selection of what?

"We'll start at Minton's then," Mrs. Mannering announced with finality. "They always have such fine fabrics, and they stock colors suitable for young ladies your age." She peered at Sarah. "Though I am sure you would prefer a ravishing gown of scarlet or ebony, daughter."

"You can choose, Mama. Your taste is so good."

"What happened to my daughter? What stranger has taken her place?" Mrs. Mannering asked so solemnly that Sarah felt her heart freeze inside her chest. Had Abigail's mother guessed her daughter had been replaced by an imposter? Would she and Micki be burned at the stake? "Surely Abigail Mannering would never blindly follow her poor old mother's advice!"

Mrs. Mannering's laughter assured Sarah she was only joking. "Certainly not, Mama," she said with new confidence. "But I *will* ask for your advice. And so shall Delphinea, I'm sure."

"Of course," Micki murmured, rolling her eyes at Sarah when Mrs. Mannering turned to address Joseph. "Our first stop will be Minton's, Joseph."

Soon the horses' hooves clattered more loudly, letting Sarah know the road was now paved with cobblestones. They were approaching town!

The scenery soon shifted to two- and three-story buildings close by one another, some of which had signs hanging over their porches: BUTLER'S LIVESTOCK SLAUGHTERING, MOSSBY'S PROVISIONS, and finally, MINTON'S DRY GOODS.

Joseph reined in the horses and handed the reins to a young boy whose job must have been to mind the carriages while ladies shopped. As Mrs. Mannering clambered down in front of them, Micki poked Sarah again, hard this time. "You've got to get us out of here, Sarah!" she hissed. "My ribs are never going to be the same!"

"I'm working on it," Sarah whispered back. "Just be patient, Micki. I'm as miserable as you are!"

That was the truth, although if pressed, Sarah might have admitted that she was also fascinated by this strange new world. What in the world were they shopping for? Why was she buying a gown?

Once inside the store, confronted by bolt upon bolt of cloth, Sarah instantly felt less displaced. This was her world, after all. She didn't feel at home in 1861, but she certainly felt at home surrounded by all this beautiful cloth.

And she decided she wasn't necessarily in any hurry to rush back to Waterview when Mrs. Mannering announced to the middle-aged man standing behind the counter, "As you see, Mr. Minton, I have brought you my daughter and my niece. We wish to see your best silks and satins," she went on with a twinkle in her eye that showed Sarah she was enjoying herself. "We three ladies need fabrics for gowns suitable for evening. In two weeks' time, we shall be dancing the Virginia Reel at the most extravagant ball in the state of Georgia!"

A ball! thought Sarah. I'm going to get to go to a real fancy-dress Confederate Ball!

As Mrs. Mannering went on to make more

specific requests to Mr. Minton, Micki took the chance to speak softly to Sarah. "I can see the wheels turning in your mind, Sarah Connell Abigail Mannering," she said knowingly. "And if you've got an eye to sticking around here in the Dark Ages for two whole weeks, in the hopes of meeting your Rhett Butler at that ball, just forget about it! I want to go back to Waterview!"

"So do I, Micki," Sarah murmured comfortingly. "So do I." But she was thinking it couldn't hurt to enjoy just one adventure as long as they were here. And two weeks wasn't such a terribly long time, not when they'd traveled more than one hundred years already!

Chapter 6

A week later Sarah and Micki sat in what Mrs. Mannering called the morning room, awaiting old Miss Colfax the dressmaker. The morning room had nothing special to do with morning that Sarah could figure out. She supposed it was called what it was because it was less formal than the main parlor, which was used for entertaining only in the evenings.

Nor was Miss Colfax especially old. Sarah had been shocked when she'd realized the woman, with her graying hair and plain, lined face, was probably no older than her own Aunt Pam. Times had certainly changed in less than a hundred and fifty years, however. Pamela Huntley was considered a vibrant woman who was always being asked out on dates; Belinda Colfax was looked upon as a spinster too old for any man to want. With marriage no longer in her own future, Miss Colfax continued to live in the home of her father, one of the county's few doctors, and in addition to ruling the widower's household, she stitched bridal and ball gowns for other women.

"Darn!" Micki muttered as her embroidery needle slipped and a drop of bright red blood appeared on her fingertip.

Sarah sighed, looking up from the pillowcase upon which she, like Micki, was embroidering an intricate garland of tiny pink flowers. "This is for the birds, isn't it?" she muttered, keeping her voice low in case Mrs. Mannering or anyone else was close enough to overhear. "The nineteenth century must have seemed like *three* hundred years to these poor girls if all they got to do was sew pillowcases."

"And for their own trousseaux!" Micki shook her head. "Didn't these people ever hear of bridal showers?"

"By the time poor Abigail and Delphinea got engaged, they could have opened a linen shop!" Sarah tossed the cloth and embroidery hoop back into the carpetbag at her feet. "Oh, where's Miss Colfax? I need something to break up this monotony!"

"I wonder what Matt and Heather and Tina

are doing right now?" Micki mused, her voice small and sad.

"They haven't even been born yet, Micki," Sarah reminded her. "It's 1861, remember?"

"You're certainly good with dates all of a sudden," Micki retorted testily. "Listen, Sarah, if you don't figure out a way to get us back to Waterview soon, it'll be too late. I'll have died of boredom!"

"You know I'm trying as hard as I can, Micki. I just hate to risk messing things up even more!"

"Then you'd better stop letting Abigail Mannering act so impulsively, Sarah," Micki told her sternly. "No more books, no more sneaking out at night. Just get us out of here!"

"Look, it's not my fault. I didn't realize Abigail wasn't allowed to read her father's books."

"No? Then why did you wait until two o'clock in the morning to go down to Mr. Mannering's library by candlelight and make off with *Murders in the Rue Morgue*?"

"Okay, Micki, so maybe I *was* pretty sure nice Confederate girls weren't supposed to read Edgar Allen Poe's horror stories, but — well, you liked reading it as much as I did, didn't you? It would have been all right if we hadn't gotten caught sneaking it back."

Micki shook her head, but she was grinning now. "I'll never forget Joseph's face when he found us in the stables!" Then she turned stern. "Lucky for us he didn't have a gun, though. He'd have shot us for sure, thinking we were horse thieves."

"We'll just have to be much more careful next time," Sarah said calmly.

"There can't be a next time, Sarah!" Micki's hushed tones were urgent. "Try to remember that this *is* the 1860s, please! These people aren't ready for girls who read horror novels and who slip out dressed in their brother's clothes and saddle up horses in the middle of the night."

"I know, Micki, and I promise to be good. Just don't forget that I didn't exactly have to twist your arm to get you to go along!"

"I'm as bored as you are, Sarah," Micki assured her. "Maybe even more bored. But when the Mannerings threatened us — " Her voice broke in shock and fear.

Sarah nodded. She'd been as terrified as Micki the day Mr. and Mrs. Mannering had sat the two of them down in the front parlor and threatened to send Micki away. Mr. Mannering, his broad cheeks red with anger above his heavy moustache and muttonchop sideburns, had spoken bluntly. "I don't know what has gotten into you two this summer," he'd rumbled in his deep baritone. "But mark my words, Abigail Mannering, if you and Delphinea continue to act oddly and get up to mischief, you will both be punished."

"You don't mean you wouldn't let us go to the ball, Papa!" Sarah had wailed, not having to fake her panic.

And that's when he'd uttered the words that had left them both more horrified than *Murders in the Rue Morgue*. "I mean that if there's one more 'incident,' not only will neither of you attend the ball, but I shall be forced to send Delphinea back home two months before schedule. If separating you two cousins is what it takes to get you to behave like well-bred young ladies, then separate you I shall!"

"Oh, no!" both of them had gasped, and Micki had quickly put in, "Please forgive us, Uncle! We'll never do anything to displease you again. We promise, don't we, Abigail?"

Sarah had seen the fear in Micki's eyes, knowing it sprang from the same roots as her own: If the two of them were split up, she might *never* be able to get them back to Waterview! "Oh, yes, Papa, I promise!" she'd vowed fervently.

Now she reached over and squeezed Micki's hand. "Don't worry, Micki. I'm sure I'll figure out a way to get us home before I'm tempted to do anything else outrageous." She cocked her head. "I'll bet that's Miss Colfax's carriage I hear. Oh, aren't you excited about seeing our gowns? I can't wait!"

"Sarah Connell, you're too much!" Micki chuckled. "Here we are stuck in some kind of awful time warp, a century away from all of our friends and families, with the Civil War practically looming in front of us, and you can still get excited about a new dress!"

They weren't just any old dresses, Micki agreed after Miss Colfax had departed, taking the gowns with her for final touches and alterations. "I couldn't picture how great they were going to look when she was just measuring and holding chunks of cloth up against us," she told Sarah. "But now that they actually look like ball gowns, wow! I never dreamed I'd be wearing a dress like that."

"I dreamed about it but never thought it would actually happen," Sarah admitted. "Gosh, do you think there's a way we could spirit them back to Waterview with us? Wouldn't that be great!"

"Don't even try it, Sarah, okay?" Micki said worriedly. "I don't want anything interfering with getting us back to good old Waterview High — gowns or no gowns. And Miss Colfax won't have them for us until the night before the ball! You mean there's no chance of our getting out of here before then?"

"I'm working on it, I promise," Sarah assured her friend, suddenly concentrating hard on taking out her embroidery and finding her place. She seriously didn't know how to get them back again and she honestly was afraid to try, but still, she didn't want Micki even suspecting that she wouldn't have dreamed of leaving the South before the ball. How could she pass up the chance to experience something so romantic? Just like Scarlett O'Hara!

"How can you sound so calm?" Micki asked. "Sarah, you just don't miss our real lives as much as I do, do you?"

"Oh, Micki, I miss Mom and Dad and the kids at school every bit as much!" Sarah assured her. "I even miss Simon and Nicole. But the fact is, we're stuck here for the time being, and everything isn't awful. I like not having lots of chores to do, and sitting on the veranda at night smelling the flowers and sewing, even if it isn't with a machine. Sure, I miss *Seventeen* and Bandit and Aunt Pam and air-conditioning and movies and — oh, just about everything! But it's not as if they're gone forever."

"You *hope*," Micki reminded her ominously. She sighed. "It's a good thing I was born in the twentieth century, I guess. I just hate tripping over the hems of these long dresses all the time, and having to lace up these old boots every day, and eating collard greens or whatever that stuff is that looks like stewed pond scum! You know something? I even miss Tasty Meat Loaf!"

"Oh, no, Micki!" Sarah laughed. "Not even that!" Then her voice turned serious. "As long as we don't have a choice, let's just try to make the best of it. Think of the entrance we'll make at the ball in those dresses. I'll bet none of the other girls will look as nice."

"Maybe not. But I'll bet they'll all know how to dance the waltz and the reel and whatever other weird dances they do around here. I'm afraid we'll look like fools, Sarah."

"Nobody could look bad in those dresses, Micki." Sarah felt a glow as she remembered the soft feel of the gown against her skin as Belinda Colfax had knelt at her feet, pinning it here and there. Because the dress was for a formal evening, Mrs. Mannering had allowed the dressmaker to cut the bodice low, almost heart-shaped, curving up to where it dipped off Sarah's shoulders in short, puffed sleeves. The fabric was watered silk in a deep, almost midnight blue, yards and yards of it falling in soft drapes in front, then gathered up to cascade in a waterfall of ruffles from the waist in the back, forming a small — and, Sarah hoped, manageable — train. And Mrs. Mannering was even letting Sarah borrow her most expensive fan, of blue silk and black lace made in Paris.

Micki's voice snapped Sarah out of her reverie. "I'm just afraid I'm going to look and act as if I'm dressed up for Halloween, Sarah. I can't get used to these crinolines and hoops. And that train! I shouldn't have let Miss Colfax do that. I know it'll be getting under my feet all night!"

"You'll look wonderful," Sarah said. She meant it, too, because Micki's gown of green taffeta trimmed with pale lemon satin was every bit as beautiful as hers. "And I'm sure I'll be able to get us back where we belong in no time at all. After all, underneath Abigail Mannering, I'm still Sarah Connell, aren't I?"

"I hope so. Sarah," Micki paused, biting her lip as if she was scared to go on.

"Hmm?"

"Well, you *are* still Sarah Connell in every way, aren't you?" Micki asked hestitantly. "I mean, you can still do the things you did in Waterview, right?"

Sarah stared at her, her embroidery forgotten. "Like what? Obviously I can't ride a bike, because there aren't any. Or go to a movie, since none have been made yet."

"I just asked a question," Micki said stiffly. "You don't have to get all snippy with me!"

"I'm not being snippy," Sarah protested, but she knew she'd snapped at Micki. She'd never told Micki of the ability she'd had to screen movies for her own pleasure, so why should she tell Micki now that she'd tried to watch *Gone With the Wind* the night before and found herself staring at the perfectly blank wall of her bedroom until she'd finally fallen asleep, exhausted from the effort. "I just don't know what you're trying to say."

"What I'm asking is, do you still have your powers, Sarah? Or is the reason you couldn't communicate with your Aunt Pam because you left all those powers back in Waterview?"

"Of course I'm the same, silly," Sarah insisted. "It's still me — Sarah — and I'm still a witch."

"You're sure?" Micki asked, sounding relieved.

"Sure I'm sure," Sarah insisted, positive the reason she hadn't been able to watch a movie was just because she'd gone back to a time before people even imagined such things as motion pictures.

"Well, that's a relief." Micki sighed. Then, as the sound of Daisy ringing the heavy brass dinner bell vibrated through the air, she added, "And that *isn't*. It's grits and greens time again."

Sarah stood up, knocking over her carpet bag as she did so, and scattering needles and skeins of embroidery floss all across the polished floorboards. "Darn!" She stared at the mess, concentrating on wishing everything back where it belonged.

Nothing happened!

Squeezing her eyes tightly closed, she put every morsel of her being into thinking, *Floss and needles, get back where you belong. In the carpetbag!*

When she opened her eyes, nothing had changed, except that Micki was giving her an odd look as she asked, "What's wrong?"

"Nothing." Thinking quickly, Sarah sniffed loudly. "I was just trying to see if I could smell what's for supper. I hope it's fried chicken and biscuits." She ducked down and quickly scooped needles and thread back into the heavy wool bag.

"How come you didn't just wish all that stuff back in the bag?" Micki asked when she'd finished.

"Now Micki, I'd decided not to use my powers lightly back in Waterview, so what makes you think it should be any different now?" Sarah asked brightly, taking her friend's arm. "C'mon. I'm starving, and I think I definitely smell fried chicken and fritter batter in the air."

"Really? Oooh, yummy! I don't even mind the greens if there's chicken, fritters, and biscuits," Micki said happily.

How happy would Micki be if she knew what had just happened? Sarah wondered as they headed for the high-ceilinged dining room. Or what *hadn't* just happened, to be more precise.

It was indeed chicken and biscuits and fritters — and no dreaded collard greens — that Daisy brought in on big ironstone platters from the cookhouse across the backyard, as soon as the girls and the Mannerings were seated.

Sarah was glad to see that Micki ate heartily. But she herself just picked at her food, her appetite gone.

If what she was afraid of might be true, how could she ever tell Micki? And what would she do? She hoped Aunt Pam somehow knew what had happened and was tracking her down this very minute. Because she and Micki were really and truly in trouble if, as Sarah suddenly feared, her magic had deserted her, and she was stuck forever in some time warp between twentieth century Waterview and nineteenth century Georgia.

Chapter 7

A delicious sense of anticipation flowed through Sarah's veins as she dressed for the ball. She was willing to bet she was every bit as excited as the real Abigail Mannering would have been.

Of course, dressing up back in the days of the Confederacy was no simple thing — nothing like popping in and out of the shower and plugging in the blow-dryer, the way Sarah might have done back in Waterview.

No, first she had to wait her turn for the bathhouse around the corner from the main house. Mrs. Mannering went first as the lady of the house. Then Micki, since Delphinea Norcross was their guest. Mr. Mannering had taken his weekly bath that morning, so Sarah was the next — and the last — in line.

Because this was a special occasion, fresh

bathwater was drawn from the well and heated for each lady. Sarah considered this an event in itself. In the two weeks she'd been at Meadowhaven, she had turned into a girl who loathed bathtime as much as she'd once adored taking hot, steamy showers. She just couldn't get used to washing in water which had already been used by Abigail's mother and Micki, but that was how they did things here, reserving fresh water for rinsing. The only thing that made it all bearable was that by the time bath day rolled around, just once a week, Sarah would have soaked in a mud puddle if necessary. She just never felt really clean after sponge-bathing herself at her bedroom washbowl in the mornings.

This afternoon, she wrapped herself in Abigail's woolen, coatlike robe, so long it fell past her ankles. In low-heeled boots, she crossed the dirt path leading from the kitchen to the bathhouse, which was conveniently located at an equal distance from the kitchen and the well.

Steam filled the old wooden bathhouse like a steamroom, so that Sarah was met by a rush of moist heat as she closed the door behind her. Bertie and Daisy were hard at work, their faces shining with exertion. Bertie's job was to bring in the tubs of boiling water from the big kitchen wood stove, while Daisy's was to add buckets of cool springwater from the well. When the narrow tin bathtub was filled almost to the brim, Daisy added fragrant gardenia-scented oil. Then she and Bertie mixed together the remainder of the cold and hot water in the vessel Bertie had used to fill the tub. Setting a small enameled pitcher within reach of the tub so Sarah could rinse herself, they left her.

Folding her robe and laying it on the wicker chair next to the bath, Sarah pulled off her boots and submerged herself in the warm, scented water.

It wasn't the comfortable bathroom of the Connell home, but Sarah knew it could have been a great deal worse. Poorer families than the Mannerings bathed in a few inches of tepid water right in the middle of their own kitchens, she knew. And they didn't enjoy the expensive luxury of French bath oils, shampoos, and soaps, either. Washing for them meant using the same crude kitchen fat and washing soda bar used for scrubbing linens. It left their skin red and raw-looking, their hair dry and lifeless.

Sarah leaned back against the rigid metal of the tub, enjoying her soak in the warm candlelight. Outside, the sun hadn't yet set, but the shed's single window was tightly shuttered for privacy. Sarah sudsed up her hair, then stood and rinsed from head to toe with fresh water before giving her hair a last rinsing with Bertie's special vinegar, water, and camomile mixture, which left her hair clean and shining. She dried herself off with the thick but coarse towels on the chair, then, donning her robe and boots once again, she made her way back to the main house.

While she'd bathed, Bertie had started a small fire in Sarah's bedroom fireplace. She sat on the small boudoir chair in front of the fireplace screen, brushing out her hair until it shone like honey. The hair, of course, wasn't Sarah's but Abigail's, a lighter shade than Sarah's own and so long it reached her waist. Though Sarah hadn't said a word to Micki, she was finding it easier and easier to look in the mirror and see Abigail quite clearly. Sarah Connell was still there, but unless she concentrated, Sarah couldn't easily make out her own familiar features. If she didn't find a way to send herself back to Waterview, would Sarah Connell one day surrender to Abigail Mannering completely?

Pushing that unwelcome thought out of her mind, Sarah thought instead of the conversation at the breakfast table only that morning.

As they'd devoured Sarah's favorite breakfast of eggs and grits with fresh salty ham and fluffy flapjacks, the Mannerings had talked about Belle Fleur, the extravagant plantation of the Jeffersons outside Atlanta, where tonight's ball would take place.

"Wait until you see Belle Fleur, Delphinea!" Mrs. Mannering was saying, her eyes wide. "Such splendor! It makes Meadowhaven look like a poor tenant farmer's spread."

"The Jeffersons must be very prosperous," said Micki in Delphinea's prim way.

"Thousands of acres passed down from generation to generation," Mr. Mannering told her. "As Cornelius Jefferson will be the first to tell you!"

"Now, John," Mrs. Mannering interjected mildly.

"I speak the truth, Amanda, and you know it. Corny Jefferson is a braggart. Always has put on airs just because he's distantly related to Thomas Jefferson and has piles of money he did nothing to earn. Hah! A peanut farmer living in a place with a high-falutin' French name. Taking people on tours of his bathroom!"

The girls almost choked on their food at that. "I beg your pardon?" Micki managed to murmur.

"Oh, yes, we've all seen it, haven't we, Abby? Proud as a peacock over Belle Fleur's indoor plumbing. Porcelain fixtures shipped from Marseilles. He had to be the first plantation owner in this area to install drainage pipes. So now the slaves are forced to carry water from the kitchen across the yard and up the stairs to fill the tub. I don't call that progress."

"Why do they carry water in?" Micki asked. "What are the pipes for?"

"To take dirty water out, of course. Pipes to carry water *in*? How would it be heated, girl? Use your head!"

"Everyone in the state knows of Belle Fleur, Delphinea," Sarah put in to cover Micki's confusion. Didn't she realize these people knew nothing of hot water heaters and running water?

"Is it far from here, Belle Fleur?" Micki asked, still looking puzzled about the water pipes.

"An hour on horseback, two by carriage," Mr. Mannering answered. "No huge distance."

Now, as she sat by the fire, Sarah thought of the four-hour round-trip journey ahead. She hoped the ball was going to be worth being jostled for two whole hours on the leather carriage seats, while trying to keep her gown from creasing.

Micki came in, as Sarah, in camisole, pantaloons, and corset, was again seated before the fire, Bertie styling her upswept hair with the hot irons she'd heated on the hearth.

"What do you think?" she asked Sarah, twirling so her full skirts and crinolines whirled.

"You look mighty nice, Miss Delphinea," Bertie said admiringly.

"Beautiful," Sarah agreed. "The yellow roses in your hair are a wonderful touch."

"Aren't they?" Micki pirouetted to the cheval glass, the better to see her reflection. "Mrs. Manner — Uh, Aunt Amanda thought of that." She looked at Sarah. "You aren't ready yet?"

"Now, Miss Delphinea, you know how fussy your cousin is about her hair. Almost done with the curling now." Bertie fashioned some more ringlets, then, putting down the iron, asked, "Do you want me to help you with your dress, Miss Abigail?"

"Oh, that's all right, Bertie. Delphinea can help me. I won't be long." Turning to Micki after Bertie had left them alone, she let out a wolf whistle. "I know who's going to be the belle of this ball."

"Oh, go on!" Micki protested laughingly in

Delphinea's soft drawl. "I'm planning to be a wallflower. At least then I won't have to do anything I'd end up doing wrong. Besides, your mother says Milly Jefferson doesn't let other girls be the center of attention at her daddy's parties."

"Then Milly's in for a big surprise," Sarah retorted confidently.

She let Micki help her into the blue gown, which clung so tightly that a special little button hook had to be put into action to join the hooks and eyes that ran up her spine.

"At least these Southern belles had the good sense to wear flat-soled boots for dancing." Micki lifted her skirts to survey her yellow calf-skin boots, laced to midshin with lime green ribbons.

"Uh-huh," Sarah answered absently as she studied her face in the mirror. Then she crossed to the fireplace.

"Now what? More curling?"

Sarah just shook her head as she rubbed her index finger in the dead embers. "I feel like something's missing," she told her friend, crossing back to the looking glass and running her finger lightly across her eyelids.

"Whatever are you doing, girl?" Micki asked

in Delphinea's stiff, shocked tones.

"It's better than no makeup at all," Sarah informed her, blending the ash into a pale gray eye shadow that turned Abigail's eyes from open and earnest to shadowed and mysterious.

"Your mama will flay you alive," Micki warned, but Sarah just shrugged, crossing back to the fireplace to pluck a lily from the vase on the mantle, shaking its red-orange pollen into her palm, then brushing the color across her cheekbones.

"Hey, give me some of that!" Micki blurted, her disapproval forgotten. "I've got to hand it to you, Sarah, you sure know how to improvise."

"I wish I knew how to improvise some lip gloss. I guess we'll just have to keep biting our lips to redden them."

"Lip gloss or not, you're going to put that Milly Jefferson to shame, Sarah," Micki predicted.

"It will do her good," Sarah said firmly as she wrapped a long black velvet shawl around her shoulders and picked up Mrs. Mannering's fan. "I can't remember the girl, but from what Papa — Mr. Mannering — says, it won't hurt her any to be taken down a peg or two. Come on, Micki, let's go get your wrap. We've got a long ride ahead, and Ah'm just dyin' to get to this ball!"

"And then you'll start thinking about nothing else but getting us back to Waterview safe and sound, right?" Micki prompted.

"Absolutely," Sarah promised as they hurried down the hall to Delphinea's room. "After all, how many grits can any girl be expected to eat?" Beneath her laughter, Sarah was serious about getting the two of them out of there. The Civil War would soon be starting and she knew from her studies that when that happened, even grits would be rationed to near starvation levels. She and Micki had to make their escape before then. Like Cinderellas at the ball, they'd soon hear the clock starting to chime.

Chapter 8

The journey to Belle Fleur was, as Sarah told Micki later, like a tour of the nineteenth century. Joseph, in his best black cotton jacket and stovepipe hat, sat high above his passengers, on the top of the carriage. Instead of the open carriage Mrs. Mannering took when she went to town, the carriage that bore them toward the Jefferson plantation was closed, something like a Wild West stagecoach, except that this carriage had an exterior painted glossy black with "Meadowhaven" in gold script on both side doors.

Inside, Sarah had to admit that the carriage was comfortable, with carpeting on the floor, cushioned leather seats, and lap robes to ward off any chills. Though the weather was balmy, air leaked in at the doors so Sarah was sure those blankets would come in handy on the ride back to Meadowhaven.

Both the Mannerings were in a festive mood. It turned out the two loved "a good waltz," as Mr. Mannering put it, and were looking forward to the night's gaiety as much as the girls.

Sarah sat next to Abigail's father, with Micki and Amanda Mannering seated opposite them. At their feet was a carpetbag which the Meadowhaven cook had packed with food — slabs of fresh-baked bread layered with sliced ham, fried chicken legs, a sack of dates and nuts, some juicy peaches, a flask of wine for the Mannerings, and one of lemonade for the girls.

Sarah had been sure she would be too excited to eat, but when Mrs. Mannering started unloading the contents of the bag halfway through the journey, she found her mouth watering.

"Just a chicken leg and a peach," she answered when asked what she wanted. "If I ate anything more, I fear I'd split my seams!"

"Eat hearty, daughter," Mr. Mannering insisted. "You'll soon dance away the pounds. And for all his wealth, we can count on Jefferson to provide no banquet. There will be enough champagne to float a battleship, but no real stick-to-the-ribs food. Nothing save platters and platters of those fancy French *hors d'oeuvres.*"

"Tell us about the restaurants you've been to, Papa!" Sarah begged. "Where were they and what were they like?"

"Let's see now. Last time I went by rail to New York City, Mr. Blythe-Higgins — he's the English gentleman who purchases our raw cotton for Queen Victoria — " he explained for Delphinea's benefit, "he entertained me at as fancy an eating spot as ever I've seen. Private rooms on Washington Square, for members only, and those members were the gentry."

He stopped and snorted. "The Yankees say we Southerners offend the notion that all men are equal, but how does the Yankee view equality if he has dining clubs where money alone cannot guarantee entrance, eh? Mark my words, the leaders of the Confederacy aren't about to be pushed around by those — "

"What did the restaurant look like, Papa, and what was served?" Sarah put in, trying to turn the talk away from the coming hostilities between North and South.

"Ah, yes, m'dear. The rooms were three in number, each holding perhaps twenty red-velvet-lined mahogany booths. The walls were of finely polished mahogany panels, gleaming in the light shed by gaslamps much like those on this carriage. In the center, where the three rooms joined, a young musician played airs by Mozart and Lizst on a pianoforte.

"The tables were arrayed with fine linens and cut-crystal wineglasses. And the platters brought to our table! A king's ransom of foodstuff, Abigail! Roast pheasants under glass, a brace of tiny quail, leg of mutton, and whole lobsters awash in the richest butter. They think nothing of eating foods from all over the globe, those Yankees. Their ports receive ships from the oceans of the world. Figs from the East, oranges from Seville, smoked eel from the London docklands."

"And desserts?" asked Micki, reaching for her second peach. "Were their pastries as flaky and tasty as ours?"

"The dessert trolley was a sweet tooth's vision of paradise," Mr. Mannering replied, patting a paunch his own love of sweets had deposited at his waistline. "I can still remember the taste of the lightest custards, of cakes layered with almonds and preserves, of strawberries dipped in sugar, pies overflowing with berries!" He shook his head. "Corny Jefferson would do well to emulate the Yankee and not the Frenchman in his pantry."

"Now, John, you know you mustn't say such things, even in jest. You know those Yankees are dishonest and arrogant. They'll realize they have overestimated their own power once Mr. Davis is declared head of the Confederacy!" Mrs. Mannering's voice rose in anger.

"I just hope Jefferson Davis doesn't end up leading our infantrymen into war," her husband said worriedly.

"Mrs. Isabel Owens came for tea last week," his wife told him, "and she says the talk in the Capital is that the Yankees will avoid a battle." She laughed merrily. "So, you see, we have no cause for worry. Our way of life is assured."

As the adults' talk turned more toward local and Montgomery gossip as repeated by Isabel Owens, Sarah exchanged a sad look with Micki. None of these people even suspected what hardships and tragedies were in store for them!

She pulled back the side curtain and watched the sun setting over the rich Georgia countryside. The carriage passed through plantation lands dotted with cotton bolls, down narrow roads lined with fir and willow trees, alongside streams with crude cabins hugging the banks, smoke curling from their crooked brick chimneys.

Now and then, they swept by a traveler's inn, where men sat and smoked pipes on the veranda, as their horses were watered and provided with fresh blankets.

It was all so beautiful, and nothing like California, where the ocean met the shore beneath rugged cliffs, where palm trees and cacti grew higher than people, Sarah thought. She'd never been to Georgia before, but she realized it probably didn't look like this anymore, either.

They rode in a silence unbroken except for the sound of the shifting of the carriage. Finally, Mr. Mannering spoke. "That's Belle Fleur, all lit up over there."

Sarah and Micki looked in the direction in which he pointed, and Sarah's pensive mood banished as her excitement blazed anew. "My word!" she exclaimed. "It's like Disneyland!"

"Like what, honey?"

"Uh, nothing, Mama. I'd just forgotten how impressive the main house really is," Sarah jabbered nervously as Micki rolled her eyes.

"Yep, it's really something," Abigail's father admitted reluctantly. "There's nothing to compare to Belle Fleur — not yet, at any rate."

"It's like something from the future, isn't it?"

Micki commented, her face turned toward the flickering lights that seemed to fill the horizon, but her eyes glinting mischievously at Sarah. "Like Tomorrowland, isn't it?"

"Tomorrowland, eh?" Mr. Mannering nodded. "I like that. But don't you go saying tomfoolery like that to Corny Jefferson, Delphinea. His head's swelled enough as it is."

Sarah glared at Micki, but she had to bite her lip to keep from laughing. How had she managed to blurt out something so stupid? And what, she wondered, would the Mannerings say if she tried to tell them about Disneyland?

Joseph turned the carriage in at a narrow cobbled drive that cut steeply out of the rolling valley toward the crest of the hill where the manor house perched. As soon as the carriage came within two hundred feet of the house, the vehicle was bathed in the light of flaming torches held by black men in uniform, who lined the drive on either side.

"Are they soldiers?" asked Micki.

"Of course not, dear. They're the Jeffersons' servants. They always wear livery for the ball."

"You are likely to see plenty of Confederate fighting men tonight, though, Delphinea," Mr. Mannering put in. "Many of the local boys hereabouts have joined up. And they wouldn't miss an opportunity to put on their fancy dress uniforms."

As the carriage turned into the circular drive immediately in front of the house, strains of a melody reached its occupants' ears. "Ah, the orchestra," Mrs. Mannering murmured. "I do love a waltz, don't you, girls?"

"Oh, yes," Micki and Sarah answered dutifully. Sarah was sure Micki would have preferred hearing that the Jeffersons were featuring dancing to the hottest music videos instead. Though she knew nothing about waltzing, either, other than that she was sure they'd done it back in dancing school when she was in fourth grade, Sarah wasn't fazed. She was sure she could fake it, and the slow, lilting music perfectly matched her romantic mood.

"Now, don't forget to make a fuss over Milly, Abigail," the older woman warned in a whisper, as the carriage halted to a stop and a servant reached up to open the door. "I know she's a silly girl with a mean streak, but she is your hostess. So please be gracious."

"Of course, Mama," Sarah said meekly, eager to climb down from the carriage and enter the great house, which was so big it might have twenty, even thirty rooms!

The double doors to the entrance hall stood open, and as they climbed the wide stairs to the veranda, Sarah glimpsed the ballroom through the tall windows to the left of the doors. It was flooded with light from a gigantic gaslit chandelier, and what she saw made Sarah feel she'd trespassed on a Hollywood studio lot by mistake. Men in uniform with scarlet and gold sashes and shining black boots swept by, dancing with bejeweled women wearing gowns of brilliant silk.

She grabbed Micki's wrist. "Look, isn't it beautiful?" she asked softly. "Like the scene in *Jezebel* where Bette Davis shows up at the ball in a red gown."

Mrs. Mannering turned back to urge them, "Come along, girls." And as they continued to stand and stare at the festive scene inside the house, she called in a louder, but still hushed, voice, "Come, Abigail. Goodness gracious, you'd think you two had never been to a party before."

"If she only knew our idea of a party is dancing to compact discs at Heather's house," Micki muttered.

Sarah chuckled. "Wearing jeans with the knees ripped out and Dodgers sweatshirts. Come on, Miss Delphinea Norcross, let's not just stand here gawkin' like a couple of time-travelers who never saw anything as awesome as this before in their lives."

Micki curtsied, her skirts sweeping across the wide step. "After you, Abigail Mannering. The Jeffersons are *your* family's friends, after all."

"Let's just hope I can somehow pick out the awful Milly I'm expected to make such a fuss over. She sounds like *Revenge of the Nerdettes*, doesn't she?"

In the entrance hall, three times as big as its counterpart at Meadowhaven, stood more servants, who took the guests' wraps and bonnets, conveying them up the wide, winding marble staircase where they could lie forgotten until the guests prepared to depart.

"Dancing in the ballroom to your left, sir," a liveried manservant informed Mr. Mannering. "Refreshments in the salon on the right."

"And where might our fine host be?" he asked. "We should like to pay our respects."

"I believe the master is taking Miss Millicent for a turn around the floor, sir."

"Shall we join the dancers, ladies?" Mr. Mannering held out his arm for his wife to take and ushered the girls ahead of him into the ballroom, which ran the entire length of the house.

A very un-Victorian "Wow!" escaped Sarah's lips as they entered the room, but luckily the loudness of the orchestra covered it. "Isn't this wild?" she whispered in Micki's ear, gazing at the scene in amazement.

"If I didn't know you were truly a witch, Sarah Connell, I'd think I was dreaming!" Micki hissed back.

The scene before their eyes was quite a spectacle. Musicians in dress coats and trousers sat behind brass music stands playing for some sixty or so dancers. On chairs against the gilded, mirrored walls sat perhaps another forty spectators, old women in modest, high-necked gowns, little girls in organdy, small boys in short pants. Not sitting but standing were small knots of women, their fans hiding their giggles as they talked among themselves, and here and there a soldier in his finest regalia.

"See any cute guys?" Sarah asked, turning away from Abigail's parents so they wouldn't hear.

"How can you think of boys at a time like this?" Micki asked.

"It's the perfect time, Micki. I mean, we're at a dance!"

"We're not just at a dance, Sarah. We're reliving history! Look in front of you. You're seeing something no one in Waterview has ever — "

"What's the matter?" Sarah asked as Micki stopped dead in mid-sentence, her eyes the size of golfballs. "Hey!" She poked an elbow in Micki's ribs. "You look like you've seen a ghost."

"I have." Micki gulped, blinked, then gulped again. "Two ghosts! Look over there, Sarah, the girl in that awful shade of pink, dancing with the older man. Then look at the soldier leaning against the far wall next to the huge oil painting. Are those ghosts — or am I seeing things?"

Sarah scanned the floor hurriedly. "Whatever are you talking — " She broke off, hand to mouth to hide her shocked intake of breath. Finally she said, "If you're seeing things, so am I. How did *they* get here?"

She was only vaguely aware that Mrs. Mannering had come up and was speaking to her as she stood, like Micki did, her astonished gaze flickering back and forth between Allison Rogers as she waltzed around the floor, and David Shaw as he stood watching the movements of the dancers.

Seeing David all dressed up like a Confederate soldier made Sarah's heart skip a beat with delight. But the sight of Allison, her expression as sour as it used to be back in Waterview, was, as Abigail might say, "a filly of a different color." When the nastiest girl in Waterview High showed up in Confederate Georgia, it was truly time to find a way back to the future!

Chapter 9

Sarah and Micki couldn't help staring at the familiar figure among the dancers. "Poor girl's taste is as bad as ever, isn't it?" Micki muttered. "The last time I saw that particular color pink, it was being poured on a tablespoon when my mom had indigestion!"

"I just can't believe it!" Sarah leaned toward her friend and kept her voice low, not wanting the Mannerings to overhear. "I kind of remember thinking David would make a wonderful Rhett Butler type. But Allison — I never would have wished *her* any place I was going to be!"

Sarah's glance flickered back toward David as the music ended. Why, she wondered, hadn't he seen her and Micki? Couldn't he see beneath the surface and recognize that they weren't really Abigail and Delphinea at all? Or hadn't he spied them yet?

Micki's low groan recalled her attention. "Don't look now, but I think she's heading this way!"

Sure enough, the girl in pink appeared to be scurrying gracelessly in their direction, her bearded, red-faced dancing partner at her heels.

"Ah, here comes Corny now!" Mr. Mannering boomed. He stepped around the girls just as the girl in pink reached them. "And Millicent, a vision in pink!"

"Abigail, Delphinea, don't you-all look sweet!" Milly Jefferson cooed in the saccharine tones of insincerity.

"Thank you, Milly," Sarah answered, relieved to see that close up, Millicent Jefferson didn't really look like Allison Rogers at all. It was the pursed, know-it-all lips which were identical, not the whole person.

"Such a purty shade of blue, Abigail," Milly went on in an unpleasantly nasal drawl. "I truly love that color on you. It does take *some* of the ruddiness out of your complexion, doesn't it? And I don't care if my mama and the rest of the society ladies hereabouts declare that midnight blue is a *coarsening* shade for a girl our ages. It becomes you, it truly does."

"And your gown is *truly* perfect for you, Milly," Sarah told her brightly. "Don't you agree, Cousin Delphinea?"

"Oh, yes, Cousin Abigail!" Micki's voice oozed honey — and, underneath, vinegar. "Wasn't I just remarking to you how much my own mother just adored that shade of pink?" Especially for her heartburn, she added to herself.

"Millicent wheedled and pleaded until we took her all the way to Richmond to see Monsieur Henri, the French dressmaker," Cornelius interjected proudly, speaking more to Mr. Mannering than to the ladies. "I needn't tell you the expense involved. All worth it to make my precious baby the prettiest girl here, of course!" As an afterthought, he tempered his boast by adding, "Not that you three aren't visions of loveliness, Mrs. Mannering, Miss Abigail, and Miss Delphinea. You are Mrs. Mannering's niece, I presume?"

"Excuse my manners, Corny. The girls were so busy fussing over one another, I didn't have a chance to introduce our guest, Miss Delphinea Norcross from Birmingham. Her papa is Amanda's brother Jasper."

"A fine man whose name is respected

throughout the Southland." Jefferson gave a theatrical little bow. As if to himself, he added, "A shame he hasn't attained greater success in the business world."

"I'll make sure my father hears of your splendid home and your hospitality," Micki said in tones so flattering Sarah doubted if anyone except herself caught the sarcasm.

"There are drinks and platters of food in the other room, John." Jefferson turned the statement into yet another boast. "Why don't you and the missus come along with me? I'm sure the girls have much to talk about amongst themselves."

"Of course we do, Papa! I'm sure Abigail and Delphinea are too excited about being at a real ball to eat a thing right now, aren't you?" Millicent asked the question as if it were a statement with no answer required. "Ah'm sure neither of you receives many invitations to parties as grand as this one. And I do declare, Delphinea, your gown's fit is so snug and perfect, I don't believe there's room for even the tiniest slice of peach cobbler, is there? You do look so much more robust than when we met in Birmingham last year."

To fill in the silence caused by the adults' departure and Micki's seething speechlessness,

Sarah commented, "I hadn't realized you two had made one another's acquaintance."

That drew forth a high-pitched squeal of laughter from Millicent, enough to make several of those nearby turn and stare. "Why, Abigail Mannering, whatever has come over you? You yourself made the introductions, remember? It was at an afternoon tea in Miss Carstairs' rooms. Don't tell me you've forgotten your old governess, Abby!" To Micki, she added, "I know the Mannerings' carriage lacks the precision suspension system Papa demands in all of ours, but I hope the journey here hasn't rattled her memories from her mind!"

"You're always such a tease, Milly!" Sarah refused to give the other the pleasure of seeing that her sharp tongue irritated. "Of course I remember. And that tall soldier against the wall." She hoped she sounded offhand. "Didn't I meet him on that occasion as well?"

"Now I know you're suffering from the vapors," Millicent smirked. "Or is it your turn to tease *me*, pretending you don't recognize your own neighbor. Robbie rode all the way from Macon, where his battalion is training, just to be here tonight. I do believe he's smitten with me," she simpered.

The simper turned to a scowl as a gawky,

rawboned youth whose hair gleamed with oil and whose evening clothes smelled of camphor approached, saying, "Ah would be mighty honored if one of you young ladies would give me the pleasure of the next dance."

"Here we are, Delphinea, monopolizing Millicent when her guests long for her attention!" Sarah chirped, grasping Micki's elbow and maneuvering her away from Millicent and the boy. "It's your night, and you must enjoy every minute of it, Milly. Come along, Cousin, we shall pay our regards to Robbie."

"Why do you suppose David's going to be glad to see us, Sarah?" Micki asked as they crossed the floor. "He's probably pretty put out about being stuck here in the Confederate boondocks without being asked if he felt like traveling. And did you wish *him* here, too?"

"Stop making me sound like a travel agent, would you? I told you I didn't wish David here, not on purpose, anyway. All I remember is thinking what a great Rhett Butler he'd make," Sarah reminded her.

She wasn't really lying, she told herself. She did remember thinking it would be nice if she and Micki lived in the South during the days of *Gone With the Wind*, and she recalled wishing that someone *like* David would be there.

But she hadn't wished for the actual David Shaw.

"I should think he'd be glad to see us, no matter what," Sarah added as they approached the soldier. "I mean, at least we've got each other. David's stuck here all by himself — and in the army yet!"

The dark-haired fellow turned and smiled happily as they reached him. "Well, he *does* look glad to see us," Micki admitted.

His first words assured her she was right. "I was hoping you two would be here!"

"You were?" Sarah stared. "What made you think we would be?"

He shook his head, still smiling with pleasure. "I remembered that your father was well acquainted with Mr. Jefferson, of course. And my mother had written that your cousin was visiting from Birmingham." He bowed low to Micki. "Miss Norcross, in the two years since last we met, your loveliness has only deepened."

"Oh, I get it. You mean you knew Abigail and Delphinea would be here!"

His response to Sarah's remark was an odd look.

"I mean, you didn't know Sarah and Micki would be here," she explained.

"Sarah and Micki? I beg your pardon, Miss Mannering, but I'm not sure — Do I know this couple?"

Sarah stepped closer. "Look, it's all right," she said softly. "I can understand your being angry, but I didn't mean to do it. It was all an accident. I was just — "

She was interrupted by a determined-looking Milly Jefferson, who was dragging her lanky dancing companion by the hand. "Poor Jebediah here is just dyin' to dance with you, Abigail," she trilled. "You ran off before he could make his request."

"Hey, can't you see I'm — " Spotting John Mannering, who had just reentered the ballroom with his wife and Cornelius Jefferson, Sarah realized she couldn't afford to be rude to her creepy hostess. Smiling as warmly as she could under the circumstances, she said, "Why, I'd love to dance, Jeb." She turned to the others. "Do keep an eye on Delphinea while I'm gone, won't you, um, Robbie?"

That'll fix that horrid Millicent, she thought as she allowed the awkward young man to lead her to the dance floor. Robbie wouldn't dare do what Milly was obviously angling for — asking her to dance — not when it would mean leaving Micki standing all by herself. Now all Sarah had to do was worry about not making a fool of herself on the dance floor.

Luckily, the dance tune was a slow waltz and Jebediah was a poor dancer. Sarah managed to follow the other dancers on the floor and her partner's feeble lead, and after that, her natural dancing abilities took over and she managed to waltz. In spite of her partner's two left feet, and the fact that she longed to be back with the others, Sarah loved the sensation of whirling around the dance floor, her fan dangling from its wrist strap, her full skirts billowing about her ankles.

"I have long hoped for the opportunity to dance with you, Miss Abigail," Jebediah confessed, his long, somewhat mulish face pinkening with either emotion or exertion.

Sarah tried to smile politely. Darn that Milly Jefferson! The last thing she needed was to be stuck with this poor excuse for a Romeo all evening! She had to find a way to get David alone so she could explain what had happened. Poor David! It was only natural for him to be confused, even dazed. What a shock it must have been to suddenly find himself more than a hundred years in the past — and in the Confederate Army!

As the music carried her past him, Sarah tried to catch David's eye. But he was playing his soldier role to the hilt, acting like the perfect Southern gentleman as he talked with Micki and Milly.

Poor thing. She wondered if he had any idea that she was responsible for his predicament. What if he never forgave her? The thought was so depressing Sarah missed the beat of the music and faltered, only to come rudely to her senses when Jebediah's boot trod heavily on her instep.

"Sorry, Miss Abigail," he apologized gruffly. "I jes' caint concentrate on the dancing when I'm so close to you. You sure are a purty li'l thing."

Great, Sarah thought wryly, of all the thousands of guys in the Confederacy, I've got to end up dancing with the 1860's answer to Gomer Pyle.

Hoping she sounded like a flirtatious belle, Sarah drawled, "Now, Jeb, Ah know you're just saying that to be mannerly. Why, anybody could see you're really Miss Millicent's beau. She's got eyes only for you."

"You think so?" he asked doubtfully. "Don't make sense her insisting I dance with you first then, does it? Not that I don't enjoy this, Miss Abigail. I mean, I *have* always wanted to do this."

"Now don't you go worryin' about mah feelings!" Sarah ordered, laughing gaily. "I can tell you've got a hankering for Milly. And I'll bet it wasn't easy for her to turn you loose. She's so thoughtful, though, isn't she? Only an excellent hostess would make such a sacrifice — parting with the man of her dreams so her friend wouldn't be a wallflower."

He didn't say anything, and Sarah wondered if she'd been laying it on too thick. She was relieved when he asked, "You think I was wrong not to dance with her?"

"Oh, no, I think you did just the right thing," Sarah assured him. "Now that she's been so unselfish, I'm sure Milly will want nothing more than to be your dance partner for the rest of the night."

"The rest of the night?" Jebediah sounded less than eager. "But I don't — "

"I know, I know," Sarah cut in before he had a chance to put into words what she knew he was thinking — that the last thing he wanted was to be stuck with Milly Jefferson for hours on end. Who would? "You don't want people thinking you're courting Milly just because her papa is one of the richest men in the state and is so *generous* to Milly's admirers."

"He is?"

There, now she'd got his interest! "Why, sure," she lied. "I heard he gave Kirby Cole a beautiful chestnut mare and two twenty-dollar gold pieces just for being so attentive to Millicent at the Coles' garden party in Greensboro last year."

"Forty dollars in gold?" Jeb's eyes bulged and Sarah was sure the hand holding hers turned even clammier as the cash register ringing in his brain wiped out any questions about the imaginary Coles and their non-existent garden party.

"That's what I heard," Sarah said firmly as the music ended.

She wasn't surprised when Jeb came to a dead stop and bowed clumsily. "I do appreciate your courtesy in dancing with me, Miss Abigail. But now I think it's only proper I should ask our hostess to be my partner for the Virginia Reel coming up."

Though Jebediah took her arm, it was Sarah who led him back to the others, scurrying to make sure Milly wouldn't manage to drag David onto the dance floor before Jeb could interrupt.

When Jebediah made a comically sweeping bow and requested the pleasure of Miss Jefferson's hand for the next dance, Milly's lips tightened into a thin line and her eyes narrowed meanly in Sarah's direction. But before the other girl could say no, Sarah took charge.

"He's such a wonderful dancer, Milly," she gushed. "You mustn't let us stop you. I believe I need a cup of punch after the exertion. Come, Delphinea, we must join my mama and papa in the other room. Won't you escort us there, Lieutenant?"

And before Milly could do a thing about it, Sarah had linked one arm through Micki's and one through the handsome soldier's and was leading them out of the room. Just before the music began, she could hear Jeb saying gruffly, "Ah have long hoped for the opportunity to dance with you, Miss Millicent."

Sarah, her feet throbbing from the beating they'd taken beneath Jeb's two left ones, winked at Micki. "Ah think for Milly, this may be a night to remember."

"To remember," Micki murmured, "*and* to regret!"

Chapter 10

Belle Fleur's formal dining room was enormous, and when she first entered with Micki and their soldier companion, Sarah's first impression was that it overflowed with both food and people.

"What a spread!" Micki exclaimed, staring openmouthed at the huge sideboard and twelve-foot-long tables piled high with food.

It was a veritable feast, and in spite of the tight-waisted gown, Sarah's mouth watered. "Let's fill our plates and take them out on the veranda so we can talk," she suggested to the others, who were eyeing the food as hungrily as she was.

She picked and chose carefully from the platters piled high with sliced ham, turkey, barbequed ribs, fresh-baked breads and muffins, vegetables, grits, potatoes, fresh fruits, and pastries. Then, a glass of punch in one hand and her plate and silverware balanced in the other, she walked through the French windows and out on the veranda.

"Is this what Mr. Mannering calls *hors d'oeuvres*?" Micki whispered to Sarah.

"Are you sure it isn't too chilly for you ladies?" Robbie asked.

Sarah shook her head. "No, at least no one will bother us. Sit down, David."

"Robbie," he corrected her gently, taking the seat across from the settee and not next to her as she'd hoped he would.

It was Micki who settled herself next to Sarah and who noted, "We know you're Robbie."

"That's right," Sarah chimed in. "Just like we're Abigail and Delphinea." The poor boy was obviously still in shock from finding himself in the nineteenth century all of a sudden, she realized. She and Micki had better go slow.

Micki met her eye and nodded. "And you're a soldier."

"That's right. I guess an awful lot has happened since the last time I saw you," he told her.

"Back in Waterview, you mean," Micki said.

He shook his head, starting to look mixed-up again. "No, at the Mannerings' during your last visit. I wasn't in the army then."

"You don't have to worry," Sarah said softly. "We're alone, and no one else can hear us. Look, we know who you are. Don't you recognize us?"

" 'Course I do. You're Miss Abigail and Miss Delphinea." He shook his head and chuckled. "How come you're pulling my leg like this?"

"David, it's us — Sarah and Micki!" Sarah's low voice was urgent. "Don't you remember? Oh, are you mad at me, is that it? You've figured out it's my fault you're here, haven't you?"

"I don't know who this David is, or Micki or Sarah, and I wouldn't say it's your *fault* I'm here. I did come partly because I was *hopin'* you'd be here, though," the young man said shyly, his green eyes warm now as he regarded Sarah.

"You mean that?" she asked, feeling her pulse quickening.

"Miss Abigail, I'd ride bareback from one end of the state to the other on the chance that I might see you when I reached my destination. But it's cruel of you to poke fun of me with all this talk of people I've never heard of."

Sarah was too thrilled and flattered to speak,

but Micki, always the voice of reason, said, "Maybe something happened to you on the way here. Maybe you hit your head or something."

"Whatever are you talking about, Miss Norcross? I'm an excellent rider. I don't fall off my mount and I don't hit my head. And there's nothing wrong with *me*. It's you ladies who don't make any sense."

"We'll have to jog his memory back," Micki told Sarah under her breath. Then, turning back to the young man, she said loudly, "The Lakers. . . . U-2. . . . tacos and enchiladas. . . . surfboards. . . . frozen yogurt!"

He just stared at her, as if she'd let loose a stream of nonsense syllables. "Is she all right?" he asked Sarah. "She sounds possessed!"

"Oh, no, no, no, she's fine," Sarah babbled. All they needed was for someone to think they'd been possessed by witches or evil spirits! "Delphinea's always had an unusual sense of humor, haven't you, Cousin?" Forcing laughter, she turned to Micki, her lips silently forming the word "laugh."

Micki managed to choke out a few chuckles. "Yes, I'm just teasing you, Robbie. Joshing in my own way." She shrugged at Sarah. How were they ever going to get David to remember who he really was?

"Whatever are you doing sitting here in the dark, Abigail?" Mrs. Mannering stood silhouetted in the French windows. "And who's that with you? A young man?"

Mrs. Mannering stepped on to the veranda, her face grim, and Sarah realized it was probably considered improper behavior for young men and women to sit on a dark porch unchaperoned in those days. But when Abigail's mother saw who it was with her daughter and niece, her features relaxed into a smile. "Why, Robbie Shaw! How good to see you. I was just asking your mother about you last week. She tells me you'll be home on leave soon."

"Yes, ma'am."

Sarah didn't hear the rest of his answer because she was too stunned by what she'd just heard. She leaned over so her lips were just an inch from Micki's ear. "Did you hear that?" she whispered. "Robbie Shaw? He's not David at all. He's a real Confederate! I'll bet he's David's great-great-great-grandfather or something. No wonder he thought we were crazy!"

Micki lost interest in Robbie Shaw after learning he wasn't a time-traveler like themselves. They should have realized something wasn't quite right, she told Sarah later. Robbie looked like the spit and image of David; there wasn't someone else there, in the way Abigail and Delphinea were there with Sarah and Micki.

Once she'd learned that Robbie wasn't David, Micki turned her full attention to her plate of food and to gossiping with Mrs. Mannering about the party. She expected Sarah to drop the young soldier like a hot potato now that he'd turned out to be a real Southern boy and not David Shaw from Waterview, California. She was surprised to note that Sarah's plate of food was deposited on the floor, practically untouched, and Sarah's eyes remained glued on Robbie Shaw's good-looking face.

"Young Jebediah Clankett appears to be totally enamored with Millicent," Mrs. Mannering told Micki. "I just saw the two of them together in the ballroom, where he was following her around with almost puppyish devotion."

"How sweet!" Micki gushed. She tried to catch Sarah's attention to give her a wink, but Sarah had eyes only for Robbie. "He seems like the perfect suitor for Milly."

"Does he?" Mrs. Mannering asked thoughtfully. "I would have supposed poor Jeb to be no match for Milly. The boy's got no backbone. Besides, he's just a poor young farmer, and I'm sure Milly and her parents agree only a young captain of industry might be considered as a beau."

"What do you think, Abigail?" Micki asked loudly.

"What do I think?" Sarah asked dreamily. "I think I'm hoping Robbie here will ask me to waltz."

"Abigail, you mustn't be so forward," Mrs. Mannering said sternly. "Why, what will poor Robbie think?"

The young man in question blushed but managed to laugh happily. "I think there's no one with whom I'd rather dance, Mrs. Mannering. Who wouldn't be flattered to have Abigail Mannering single him out as a dancing partner?"

"Why aren't you and Papa on the dance floor?" Sarah asked, getting to her feet. "Let's go find him, Mama. Then we can all waltz."

"Delphinea and I shall accompany you back inside," Mrs. Mannering told her. "But I don't know whether we'll dance. The last I saw of your father, Mr. Jefferson was taking him on a tour of the stables to see their two new foals."

"Well, then, you and Delphinea can keep each other company and watch to see if Lieutenant Shaw and I make the most handsome couple on the floor. It will be so exciting to dance with a man in uniform," she added for Robbie's benefit alone.

" 'It will be soooo exciting to dance with a man in uniform!' " Micki mimicked when she and Sarah were back in Abigail's bedroom at Meadowhaven much later that night. "Really, Sarah, you sounded like something out of a bad movie. I'm surprised you didn't start admiring his muscles!"

"Well, aren't we in a jolly mood? I'm sure someone might have asked you to dance, Micki, if you hadn't gone around sulking all night."

"I was *not* sulking," Micki retorted. "Besides, I didn't want to dance, not if dancing meant doing the stupid waltz and the ridiculous reel."

Sarah shook her head pityingly. "You just have no sense of history, do you? Or romance, either. If you'd just loosened up, Micki, you could have had as wonderful a time as I did."

"I figured you were loose enough for the both of us. The way you were hanging on him all night! Sarah, girls didn't act that way back then."

"This *is* back then, remember? And Robbie didn't find my attention such a pain."

"Of course not. He's probably not used to females being so forward like that. Probably thought he'd died and gone to heaven. 'Ah do declare, Looootenant Shaw is the most mah-velous dancer.' As they used to say not quite so long ago, gag me with a spoon!"

"What in the world's gotten into you, Micki? Are you jealous? Is that it?"

"No, of course I'm not jealous. Or maybe I am, just a little. But mostly I'm just ticked off. I hate it here, Sarah. Sure, it's been fascinating to see how people really lived back on the plan-tation, and the Mannerings are nice as can be, and the food at the party wasn't half bad. But face it, I'm a fish out of water. Can't you imag-ine how I felt, watching you act as if you were having the time of your life when all I want to do is go home?"

"Oh, Micki, I'm sorry!" Sarah, who had been waltzing around the room in her long white nightgown, stopped and sat next to her friend on the canopied bed. Reaching over, she squeezed Micki's hand. "It wasn't very nice of me to ignore you as much as I did after meeting Robbie, was it? It's just that — Oh, Micki, it's so romantic! He really truly swept me off my feet."

"Great. Now how about putting your thinking cap on and figuring out how to sweep *us* back to Waterview High?"

"I'm trying to figure something out, Micki. How many times do I have to tell you that?"

"Let's try right now, Sarah," Micki suggested, her eyes alight with hope. "Even if we end up in the American Revolution or something, it can't be much more primitive than this."

"Oh, no, Micki, this isn't a good time at all," Sarah insisted. "I — I'm too tired to concentrate my energy enough to send us anywhere. That party was just exhausting! After I've rested up, I'll try something."

"Uh-huh." Micki's expression was as suspicious as her voice. "And when would that be?"

"Oh, I don't know," Sarah answered airily. "Maybe in a week or two."

Micki jumped up off the bed. "Sarah Connell, I don't believe it! You're stalling just because Robbie Shaw's going on leave next week and coming to stay with his folks, aren't you?"

"Of course not, Micki," Sarah insisted. Then, trying to be more truthful, she added, "I do want to see Robbie again, but I really am tired. I don't want to fritter away whatever magic powers I've got left."

"What do you mean, whatever powers you've got left?"

"Well, I — I can't do some things I could do at Waterview, Micki. I tried after you asked me about that — and some things worked and some didn't. My magic is sort of hit or miss now."

"Oh, no!" Micki didn't try to hide her panic. "Sarah, what if it's waning all the time? Don't you see? You can't wait to try to get us back there. If you wait and your powers fade completely, we'll never get out of here! I can't face a life of eating grits! Come on, Sarah, try something now! Don't risk our being lost in time like this, just so you can see some boy again!"

"Micki, I don't want you to be unhappy. And I know it's my fault you're stuck here in the first place. Look, why don't I try to send you back right now? We'll just have to hope for the best."

"What do you mean, send *me* back? What about you?"

"Oh, I just figured it might be easier to send us back one at a time, that's all."

"That isn't all, though. Oh, Sarah, you do want to stay here because of him, don't you?"

"Just a few more weeks, Micki. Then I'll try to get myself back to Waterview."

"Forget it," Micki said firmly. "I'm not going any place without you, Sarah. If you tried sending me back alone, anything could go wrong. Why, I could end up in outer space with only satellites for company, or back in some cave wearing a leopard-skin leotard and gathering nuts for dinner — and you'd never even know! No way, Sarah. When I say good-bye, it's got to be with you right by my side."

"Then you're just going to have to wait. I can't leave Robbie now. Micki, someday someone will come into your life and you won't be able to just walk away. That's how I feel about Robbie," Sarah said dramatically. "Couldn't you see the sparks fly between us? Like Scarlett O'Hara and Rhett Butler! Oh, Micki, don't you have any romance in your soul?"

"Haven't *you* got any sense at all, Sarah? Scarlett O'Hara and Rhett Butler! Give me a break! My best friend doesn't care how miserable I am just because she's got a crush on some soldier and she tells me it's *my* problem?"

"I did offer to do what I could to send *you* back alone," Sarah reminded her.

"Thanks a bunch," Micki said sarcastically. She got to her feet. "Okay, Sarah, two weeks. After that, you can send me back and you're on your own."

"You mean it? You'd actually go without me?" Sarah asked in surprise.

Micki nodded. "If I've got no other choice, I'll give it a try. Why not?" She crossed the door as Sarah watched, speechless. "Don't look so shocked," she said just before she left. "At this point inventing the wheel is a much more attractive proposition than standing by while you turn into a helpless, hopeless Southern belle."

"I'm not hopeless!" Sarah shouted at the closing door. But no sooner was she alone than she positioned herself in front of the mirror, watching her reflection in the flickering gaslight as she practiced cooing, "Ah confess, Lieutenant Robbie Shaw, this past week was the longest in all my young days."

Not bad, she congratulated herself as her mirror image demurely ducked its head and peeked up coquettishly from beneath lowered lids. Abigail Mannering, Ah do believe you've got what it takes!

Chapter 11

The next few days were miserable ones for Sarah. Micki gave her the cold shoulder, keeping to herself or hanging out with Daisy and Bertie in the kitchen. To Sarah, every day might have had a hundred hours. There wasn't much to do except wait for the next day. No records or CDs to play, no radios to flick on, no TV shows, no movies on tape, no magazines — how did these people stand it? Sarah did what she could to help Mrs. Mannering with Meadowhaven's garden, weeding, cutting flowers, and just generally making herself useful. But she suffered in the heat from her heavy clothing.

One day, out of longing for the California beaches as much as anything else, Sarah slipped out the back door in her robe, carrying a blanket. She found what she hoped was a secluded place and stretched out in the sun, rolling up her pantaloons and pulling down the straps of her camisole so she'd get an even tan. She knew she looked best with some color, and she was determined to be tanned and glamorous for Robbie.

Unfortunately, John Mannering discovered her, sound asleep, when he was walking out to check on some seedlings in one of the fields.

"Abigail, what's happened?" he shouted. "Are you all right? Speak to me, daughter!"

"Just catching a few rays," Sarah answered groggily before she realized where she was and what she was doing.

"Talking gibberish . . . It must be sunstroke!" Mr. Mannering exclaimed, as if to himself. Suddenly Sarah felt herself lifted from the ground, blanket and all, as Mr. Mannering ran toward the house with her in his arms.

"Whatsamatta?" Sarah tried to talk, but her face was mashed into the rough serge of his jacket. What in the world was he doing with her?

"Quick, Bertie, send one of the stable lads for Dr. Colfax! I believe Abigail is suffering from sunstroke."

"But I was just — " In vain, Sarah tried to

explain, but Mr. Mannering was moving too fast, taking the stairs two at a time, for her to speak.

"John, what is it?" she heard Mrs. Mannering rush into the upstairs hallway, her voice tight with worry.

"I found poor Abigail out back like this! She must have been going to the bathhouse and been overcome by the sun," he explained, bearing Sarah into Abigail's bedroom. "Her robe was lying next to her. She must have ripped it off in her delirium."

"Oh, dear! Has someone gone for the doctor?"

"I had Bertie send one of the lads," he said, gently depositing Sarah's limp form on the bed.

"Look, I'm fine, honest I am," Sarah tried to sit up and explain. "I just wanted to lie down in the sun to — "

"Lie back, Abigail." Mrs. Mannering's voice was gentle as she pushed Sarah back onto the pillows and asked her husband, "Could you get me a damp cloth for her forehead, please, John?"

"What's the excitement?" Sarah heard a voice immediately recognizable as Micki's "Delphinea drawl."

"Your cousin's been overcome by the sun," Mrs. Mannering answered. "I'm sure she'll be all right, but we've sent for Dr. Colfax. She's delirious, I'm afraid."

"She is?" Micki sounded suspicious.

"Her father found her lying outside in her undergarments!" Mrs. Mannering sounded scandalized. "And just now she tried to tell me she was lying there trying to get burned by the sun! You know she'd never do something as mad as that, Delphinea. Abigail, so proud of her ivory skin, the finest complexion in the county, exposing herself to the sun's rays! My goodness, I hope her father found her before she soaked any of them up. She'll have ruined her complexion!"

Sarah pushed herself up once again to protest. Then, even as she opened her mouth, she realized what Mrs. Mannering was saying. Of course Abigail would never have intentionally tried to get a suntan. Southern ladies prided themselves on their pallor. Didn't they even use parasols to shield themselves from the sun? And she was sure to be punished severely if the Mannerings even suspected she might have purposely stretched out in her underwear, even though those garments covered her as much as the clamdiggers and halter top she might have worn to the mall back in Waterview.

"Water!" she rasped harshly, rolling her eyes back in her head as she fell back against the pillows. "Water, please!"

"Oh, Delphinea, could you pour a little in a glass for me? And here comes John with the cloth for her forehead."

Though she felt awful about upsetting the Mannerings and making the doctor rush over to Meadowhaven, Sarah remained limp and kept her breathing shallow until old Dr. Colfax had examined her and assured the Mannerings she was in no danger.

"Just give her plenty of cool liquids and nothing but light foods," he prescribed as he was closing his black bag to leave. "A touch of heat prostration, I'd say. Nothing serious, though she'll have to use plenty of powder to cover the ruddiness in her face for a week or so."

Great, Sarah thought, I try to look gorgeous for Robbie and do the exact thing I shouldn't have! As soon as the door closed and the room was bathed in silence, she jumped up and ran to the mirror to gauge how much damage she'd done.

"What's the matter — couldn't you find any suntan lotion?"

Sarah wheeled around to see Micki sitting on the chair by the fireplace, coolly working on her embroidery.

"I don't have the slightest idea what you're talking about," Sarah said stiffly.

"Water!" Micki croaked. "Water!" She laughed. "If they had a Confederate Oscar, I'd nominate you."

"Was I that bad?" Sarah laughed. She should have known she couldn't fool Micki. "I never dreamed anyone would catch me, Micki. And I completely forgot Southern belles were obsessed with *not* getting tanned!"

"At least Mr. Mannering stumbled over you before you turned bronze," Micki told her. "You're just a tiny bit pink."

"Not the color of Milly Jefferson's horrid dress, I hope." Sarah peered at herself in the glass, then returned to bed. She didn't want to get caught up and about if one of the Mannerings suddenly returned. "I didn't mean to scare everybody, Micki. But when I realized I couldn't possibly come up with an explanation, well — "

"You decided it was better to just go with

the flow," Micki finished for her.

"You won't tell, will you?"

"Just because I'm not crazy about the way you're acting lately doesn't mean I'd try to get you in trouble. Even if I wanted to, I'd be afraid your punishment might mean my being sent to Birmingham. And like I told you, when I leave here, it's not going to be alone, not if I can help it."

"Oh, Micki, you're the best friend a girl ever had! Have I been terribly selfish?"

Micki put down her embroidery and came to sit at the foot of the bed. "I just wish you were as eager to get back to Waterview as I am. Don't you miss the twentieth century, Sarah? What about your mother and father and Simon and Nicole? And Matt and Kirk and Tina and Heather and —" She broke off, blinking back tears. "We've been gone so long, Sarah. I'm just afraid we'll never get back!"

"I do miss everyone. And everything," Sarah admitted. "With you avoiding me the last few days, I've been miserable, Micki. What I wouldn't give for some microwave popcorn and a rerun of *Leave It to Beaver*! You're right, Micki. I shouldn't risk losing all that because of some boy."

"You really feel that way, Sarah? You mean you'll try using your powers?"

Sarah nodded. "Right now. Close your eyes and take my hand, Micki, and don't say anything. Not a word."

"Okay. Oh, I hope this works!" Micki whispered fervently, her hand tightly gripping her friend's.

I wish Micki and I were back in Waterview and not stuck in Confederate Georgia! Right now! Sarah put every fiber of her being into making the wish, wishing it over and over again, concentrating all of her energy into wishing the two of them back through time and space. She heard the muffled shouts of the men working in the fields and the clatter of the pots and pans from the kitchen out in back, and she concentrated all the harder, trying to shut out the sounds so her mind was aware of nothing except her wish.

She could tell nothing was happening. She couldn't do it!

She heard a knock at the door and dropped Micki's hand as if it were a burning coal. "Can I come in?" Bertie's voice called liltingly.

"Lie down and close your eyes!" Micki hissed. "Come on in, Bertie!"

"I just brought some fresh lemonade for the

patient. And for you, too, Miss Delphinea. How she doin'?"

"Oh, um, better, I think," Micki stammered. "She woke up before and we talked a little. She knows where she is now and that she's all right."

Sarah opened her eyes to see Bertie standing over her, a look of concern on her face and a frosty goblet of lemonade in her hand. "Oh, Bertie, how nice of you," she said warmly, reaching for the glass. "I'm so embarrassed at causing everyone so much worry," she said truthfully.

"We all's just glad you're all right. I'll bring some soup up for Miss Abigail later," Bertie told Micki. "Will you be eating with the family, Miss Delphinea?"

"Please dine with my parents, Cousin. Don't feel you must coop yourself up here with me," Sarah encouraged her.

"If that's what you wish, Abigail. Yes, Bertie, I'll have my supper downstairs. And thank you for the lemonade."

The minute Bertie was gone, Micki turned to Sarah. "Well, what happened?" she said.

Sarah shook her head. "Bertie knocked at the door before I really had a chance to give it a try," she said.

"Well, let's try again."

"I can't, not now." Sarah sighed. "Let me spend a couple days trying to gather my energies, Micki. I'm not stalling, I promise. I just want to make sure I do it right."

"I believe you," Micki assured her. "Darn it, though! I really had my hopes up for a minute there."

"Don't worry, we'll get back. Trust me."

Not until Micki had gone downstairs to the dinner table did Sarah allow herself to feel the full disappointment of her failure. She couldn't tell Micki that she didn't know why her powers had failed her. She'd fibbed about Bertie's interrupting them. By the time the knock at the door came, Sarah had already realized her attempt was unsuccessful.

What if I'm not a witch anymore? she wondered. Could she do anything? She gazed at the thin trickle of light seeping between the drawn drapes at the window. Open, drapes, she wished with a heart-wrenching effort. Slowly — but surely, the drapes slid apart. "I haven't lost *everything*!"

She slipped from the bed and crossed to the window, standing and staring up at the heavens. The sky was still bright. "Are you out there somewhere looking for me, Aunt Pam? Can you help me find whatever power I need to get back to all the people and places and things I love?"

Feeling lost, and lonelier than she had since this whole misadventure began, Sarah gazed at the sky until she was too tired to stand any longer. Then she headed back to bed, detouring to scoop up Clementine, who was dozing on the hearth.

She lay the cat on the pillow next to her and curled up with her head against its chest. To the comforting sound of Abigail's pet's purring, Sarah finally fell into a dreamless sleep.

Chapter 12

The Shaw's small plantation, Pine Manor, was less than ten miles from Meadowhaven, so it was only natural Robbie would stop by on his way home. What didn't seem natural to Sarah was that he didn't ask for her.

It was at the dinner table, as she and Micki tried to pick only the vegetables out of steaming tureens of rabbit stew (which Micki later likened to "being served Bugs Bunny with a baked carrot in his mouth") that John Mannering told his wife, "Robbie Shaw's home on leave. Stopped by the stables to say hello."

"The stables!" Sarah exclaimed. "He didn't come to see me?"

"I don't know what has gotten into you lately, Abigail!" Mrs. Mannering chided her.

"You know better than that. Why, it wouldn't be proper for a young man to just drop in on a lady, especially not when he's covered with the grime of a journey."

"Oh, of course not, Mama," Sarah said meekly, swallowing a sigh. All these stupid rules and regulations! Everybody was so prim and proper you practically had to make an appointment just to say hello.

"He asked to be allowed to come to call tomorrow afternoon," Mr. Mannering went on in his steady expressionless way. Then, with a sly smile in Sarah's direction, he added, "Seemed to me it was our young Abigail he was most interested in seeing."

"Did you tell him yes, Papa?" Sarah asked eagerly.

"Couldn't see the harm in it. Your cousin Delphinea should be a reliable chaperone. Can't see there's anything wrong with three young people sitting on the veranda, speaking of this and that."

"Thank you, Papa." Sarah wondered what he'd say if she told him that in another century, people her age and Robbie's would be going off on dates alone and not coming home again until hours and hours past the Mannerings' bedtime. There was no denying living in the past had its romantic aspects. On the other hand, it could be a colossal drag.

"He'll be coming by sometime after midday," Abigail's father said in a tone that marked the end of that conversation. "Now, why are you young ladies just picking at your stew? I thought rabbit was one of your favorites, daughter."

"I — I'm just not terribly hungry for hot food tonight," Sarah said apologetically. "It must be the heat. But what I did eat is delicious. The rabbit's just right, isn't it, Cousin?"

"Tasty," Mick agreed, unconsciously wrinkling her nose in distaste. "But I seem to be off my food today, too. I think you're right, Abigail. It's this warm weather."

"You may be excused from the table then," Mrs. Mannering told them. "The warm peach tartlets with hot custard sauce for dessert certainly hold no appeal."

Demurely, Sarah and Micki excused themselves and went to Sarah's room — but not before stopping out back at the cookhouse and cadging some tarts to smuggle upstairs, piping hot from the big bake oven and *almost* too good to eat.

The following day Sarah was in more of a stew than the rabbit had been, trying to decide which of the day dresses in her wardrobe was most flattering. When Micki came to fetch her for breakfast, Sarah was still in her night-clothes and her bed was piled high with outfits.

"It's nice to see how consistent you are, re-gardless of the century." Micki grinned at the heap of clothing. "It doesn't seem all that long ago Nicole was lecturing you on the proper way to care for someone else's clothes."

"But these *are* my clothes," Sarah protested.

Micki shook her head. "They're Abigail Man-nering's clothes, remember? And I suppose that if we ever get out of these bodies, Abigail and Delphinea are going to come and reclaim them. The Civil War hasn't begun, Sarah. Don't you think Abigail might prefer it if her dresses didn't look as if they'd been through the war?"

"Just help me decide what to wear, then I'll hang them up, every single one," Sarah prom-ised. "What do you think?" She held up a simple dress of pale rose and white gingham with tight, fitted sleeves and a row of bows down the front, from neck to ankle. "Too boring, isn't it?"

"I just don't think it's you, Sarah. Abigail, maybe. You, unh-uh."

"How about this one?" Sarah lifted a green

and yellow tarlatan from the pile and held it up.

"I like the way the skirt falls in tiers," Micki noted. "But isn't that material a little — "

"Preppy? I thought so, too. Okay, here's my final choice."

"I like that," Mick said admiringly of the lilac broadcloth sprigged with tiny blue and yellow flowers. "It's cheerful."

"Then this is it," Sarah said firmly even as she ducked to slip the yards of fabric over her head. "Would you hook me up and tie my sashes?"

"It's so much trouble just getting dressed," Micki complained as she fumbled with the little fasteners. "I can't believe I took things like zippers and Velcro and drawstring waists for granted all my life."

"And sandals," Sarah added, wincing as she sat on the bed and pulled on her boots. "And think of the uniforms! Can you imagine poor Robbie having to ride a sweaty old horse dressed in a heavy jacket buttoned up to his chin?"

"Sarah, promise me one thing," Micki said, her tone serious, as she helped her friend pin up her hair before going downstairs. "Promise you won't lie to me and say you can't get us back if you can, all right? If you really decide you want to stay here — she rolled her eyes — "and goodness knows you're stubborn enough that I know you might end up doing just that, then I'll go on my own, all right?"

"I thought you were afraid you'd end up with the Flintstones," Sarah reminded her.

"At least I'd have tried," Micki said solemnly. "I'd know I tried to get back where I belong."

"I promise," Sarah said. "But don't count me out, please. Much as I really feel at home here a lot of the time, I don't know if I'm ready to say good-bye forever to pizza, bacon cheeseburgers, and fries!"

But being stuck in the past didn't seem like such a rotten option when Sarah was reunited with Robbie that afternoon. She'd forgotten just how much he looked like David Shaw, how adorable his chivalrous, old-fashioned manners were, how his green eyes lit up when he looked at her, making her feel like the prettiest belle in all the South.

The Mannerings joined the three younger people on the wide, shady porch, so Sarah and Micki were mostly silent, listening as the others discussed various local folks and relatives — old Barnett Higgins, who was one of Jefferson Davis's closest advisors; the Shaws' cook Nellie; Abigail's brother Sam and his chances of remaining a bachelor much longer; and Robbie's sister Lucy.

"I spent some time with Sam down in Montgomery the other week," Robbie remarked. "He's hankerin' for hostilities to start. Says he's ready to show them Yankees."

"Oh, Robbie, do you really think the North will fight us?" Mannering asked with worry.

"Looks that way, now that Lincoln has been elected," Robbie admitted reluctantly. "The generals say the man will never recognize the Confederacy. Thinks we're a bunch of upstart secessionists underminin' the common good."

"Shouldn't the South do more to prepare?" Sarah asked, knowing darned well they should have.

"I do beg the ladies' pardon." The handsome soldier's face reddened. "Forgive me for being so crude as to distress you with talk of war."

"But it's important to us, too," Sarah protested. "Why shouldn't — ?"

"Abigail, such things aren't for the fairer sex to concern themselves with," Mr. Mannering warned. "It's not well-bred for a woman to discuss politics." To Robbie alone, he said, "Our

Abigail is often too outspoken for her own good."

"I like a girl who's sometimes daring," Robbie said, smiling at Sarah with such affection she forgot about ever getting back to California.

Mr. Mannering shook his head resignedly. "First they think it's a woman's place to talk about a man's war; next thing you know, they'll think they should be allowed to vote."

"Well, why shouldn't we?" Sarah protested. "Certainly woman are as capable of choosing as men."

To her horror, they all — even Mrs. Mannering — laughed as if she'd made an outrageous joke. And she was about to keep on talking when Robbie, no doubt sensing that she was capable of getting herself in trouble, said suddenly, "Why, I've forgotten to invite you all to dinner tomorrow evening. Lucy and her husband will be coming all the way from West Virginia to visit while I'm at home. Say you'll come! My mother is counting on it."

"I've got a crop ready to come in — " Mr. Mannering began doubtfully, but for once, to Sarah's joy, his wife asserted herself and cut in.

"Come, John, say yes. We haven't shown poor Delphinea much of our county's social life during her visit, and I'm sure the ball at Belle Fleur is already a distant memory."

"Since Abigail believes you are as capable as I am to choose, my dear, I'll give in to your wishes this once," he agreed as Sarah feigned a cough to hide her triumphant smile.

"Wonderful! Mother will be so pleased to see you, as will Lucy and Martin." Robbie pulled a heavy watch on a chain from his pocket and flipped up the cover. "And now I must be making my good-byes."

Sarah knew better than to protest and did her best to smile calmly as he stood and bowed. Teenaged daughters were clearly expected to be seen and not heard, and she dared not risk saying a word which might topple the plans for the next evening.

Still, the afternoon had been far from what she'd expected. "Tell me," she asked Micki later when they were seated in the morning room trying to draw a still life of Clementine curled on a wingback chair, sketching being a hobby they'd been encouraged by the Mannerings to pursue, "was our little get-together this afternoon what folks in these parts and these times would consider a date?"

"I do believe so, Abigail," Micki answered in her best Delphinea voice.

"So when do he and I get to be alone?"

"Ah believe a young Southern gal's reputation could be besmirched by too much forwardness on her part, Cousin."

"Besmirched?" Sarah laughed. "Are you reading *Thirty Days to a Bigger Vocabulary* or something? Where in the world do you dig up this lingo?"

"If you *must* know, I'm so beside myself with nothing to do that I borrowed some of your 'mama's' romance novels."

"I thought we weren't allowed to read."

"*Murders in the Rue Morgue*, no. Mushy love stories where no woman ever asserts herself or gets besmirched, yes."

"They sound dreadful!" Sarah giggled.

"Oh, mah deah, you wouldn't believe all the fainting and swoonin' and carryin' on."

"Fainting and swoonin' and carryin' on? That's unbelievable. I mean, when does anyone get to be alone long enough to even kiss?"

"Come back to the nineteenth century, pal. Kissin' a boy is definitely besmirching."

"You're kidding!"

"So help me. All that fainting and swoonin' and carryin' on is all right, but no kissing until the wedding."

"The wedding?" Sarah squeaked. "Micki, I'm

140

just — I mean — Abigail's just seventeen!"

"That's a good marryin' age in these here parts, Sarah. Seriously. You've got more of a chance of ending up at the altar with Robbie Shaw than you do of going on a date or stealing a kiss."

"You've got to be kidding! I can't get married. Micki, I'm a *kid*! I've got too much to do before I'd even think about getting married!"

"Like what? Be a fashion designer? Maybe back in Waterview, but not here. And not now. Here and now, there's nothing to do — except sketch and sew and maybe keep a diary or learn to play the piano. So if you're thinking about stayin' on here in the Confederacy, you'd better start picturin' what your life's going to be like. Women's liberation for Abigail and Delphinea meant unlacing their corsets at the end of the day."

"Robbie's not like that." Sarah rushed to his defense. Then she remembered how he hemmed and hawed and apologized just for letting the word "war" reach their ears. "But," she added quickly, "that still doesn't mean I'm fixin' to stay."

That decision, she went on to add only to herself, was one she still wasn't ready to make.

Chapter 13

From the moment the Mannerings' party arrived at Pine Manor, Robbie's sister Lucy made no secret of the fact that she thought Abigail Mannering was simply wonderful. Sarah wished she could return the feeling.

Almost as soon as Lucy and her husband Martin Bannister were introduced, the doll-like little blonde woman attached herself to Sarah. "Oh, my, what a beautiful dress you're wearing!" she gushed, reaching out to fluff up the ruffled tiers on the skirt of Sarah's silvery blue brocade dress. "And real silk! Wherever did you find such a talented dressmaker in these parts?"

"Oh, um — " Sarah faltered. Was this dress yet another example of Miss Colfax's artistry?

Luckily, Amanda Mannering came to her

rescue. "John had that made for Abigail when he traveled to Raleigh last year to meet a cotton dealer," she answered for her daughter.

"Ah just love *peau de soie!*" Lucy bubbled. "Oh, deah, now I feel so drab!" She twirled to better display the sweeping skirt of her own frilly organdy frock, making it perfectly clear that she felt no such thing. "I say, Abigail, you have just blossomed since last I saw you. That was — what? — at least three years ago, wasn't it? Just after Martin and I were wed. You do remember meeting Abigail then, don't you, Martin? Just a little bit of a thing. And now look at her!"

"A beautiful dress only enhances your beauty, Miss Mannering," Martin Bannister said politely, but he had eyes only for his pretty, petite wife, who was so girlish she made Abigail feel like a dull old crone.

"And Delphinea, too," Lucy twittered on. "Ah'll bet you break all the boys' hearts back home in Birmingham. What a lucky man my darlin' brother is to have two such lovely dinner guests!"

And, though Sarah would have much preferred to sit by Robbie, who looked handsomer than ever in his fancy dress uniform, while she sipped her before-dinner punch, Lucy's little hand firmly grasped her elbow and pulled her to sit down on a stiffly uncomfortable loveseat off by itself in one of the front parlor's windowed alcoves.

"However do you stand it here, Abigail?" Lucy asked in the same chirping tones. "You must come to West Virginia to visit us soon. Martin and I find no end to the social life there. Teas and dances, poetry readings, recitals, with so much to do, there is never a dull moment!"

"It sounds exhausting," said Sarah, forgetting how she complained to Micki that at Meadowhaven there was nothing to do.

"Not at all, Abigail. It's constantly amusing. And, of course, Martin's position demands a great deal of social attendance."

"His position?" Sarah repeated, not quite sure what Lucy meant.

"As part of the governor's inner circle, you see. Martin is expected to mingle freely with the state's great mercantile chiefs and wealthy plantation owners. The governor insists on being kept up-to-date, on an informal basis."

"Up-to-date on what issues?"

"Oh, that's not for me to know!" Laughing gaily, Lucy gave a pert little shake of her head.

"That's a man's domain, isn't it? Business and such?"

"You mean you don't know exactly what your own husband does?" Sarah asked in surprise.

"Of course not, Abigail!" Lucy sounded momentarily hurt at the judgment implied by Sarah's tone. "It's surely none of my concern to stick my nose into such affairs. And even if I did" — more merry laugher — "it would be more than my little head could take in, I fear. I keep quite busy with my own interests."

"What are you interested in?" Sarah asked eagerly, hoping to find a common bond. "Clothing, I'm sure. I'd like to be a designer myself someday."

"A designer? A dressmaker, you mean? Why, surely, Sarah, your parents will provide a dowry to spare you any work. Dressmaking is a rather *common* occupation, I feel."

"Dowry?" Sarah cautiously pronounced the unfamiliar word.

"Of course, Abigail. The money and goods your family gives to the man who chooses to marry you."

"Oh, of course," Sarah mumbled, hoping she didn't betray her sense of outrage. She'd forgotten all about dowries, though now she remembered reading about them. The idea that anyone should be rewarded for taking a marriageable daughter off a family's hands was repellent to her. But then, what else could a girl expect? She wasn't expected, or allowed, to pursue a career. Looking away, she smiled at Robbie, who was studying her adoringly. Or, Sarah wondered, was he just calculating how many Confederate greenbacks she might be worth?

"So, what are your interests?" she asked Lucy.

"Oh, so many things!" Lucy reverted to her usual bubbly self. "I paint watercolors, for my own pleasure only, of course," she added with sniff, implying that the desire to be an actual artist was another "common" pursuit. "And I work with the Ladies' Auxiliary one day a week, stitching uniforms for our troops. I also do my own stitchery — I have half-finished a coverlet in only four months! I write poetry at times, though I would never dare show another soul my silly ramblings. Naturally, I tend to the staff to make certain they are carrying out their daily chores. Dressmakers' visits, my rose garden, entertaining for tea — my days are never empty."

Sarah murmured noncommittally, thinking it

sounded even more dreary than life at Meadowhaven, where she was at least left mostly to her own devices.

"I shall ask Martin to speak to your parents to see if you can visit soon. We so enjoy having a guest. And our whist parties are such a treat. I hope you play cards."

"I've played blackjack once or twice."

"Blackjack?" Lucy's horrified look showed that blackjack was *not* for ladies. Then she laughed merrily. "Oh, Abigail, you're teasing me! Of course a young girl such as yourself wouldn't play such a game. Why, next you'll be insisting you shine at billiards!"

"What's wrong with — " The sound of a gong stopped Sarah's tongue.

"Let's sit side by side at dinner, so we can talk some more!" Lucy said firmly as she jumped to her feet.

"What a wonderful idea," Sarah agreed wanly, wondering how she'd be able to eat and fend off Lucy's silly chatter at the same time. How, she wondered, had Robbie ever gotten such an airhead for a sister?

She didn't manage to slip away from Lucy, but she did maneuver a bit so Robbie sat on her other side at the big lace-covered table.

"I'm pleased to see you and Lucy get on so

well," Mrs. Shaw, Robbie's widowed mother commented from her seat at the table's foot, opposite her son-in-law at the head. "I believe the difference in your ages was all that kept you two from being bosom friends in the past."

"Four years seems like such a lot when one girl is eleven and the other fifteen, but so little when seventeen and twenty-one are reached," Lucy remarked, leaving Sarah amazed that something intelligent could come out of her mouth.

"Robbie was telling us earlier that Mr. Bannister has guaranteed him a position with the West Virginia governor after he's finished his service for the Confederacy," Micki, across the table from Sarah, said. "Isn't that grand, Abigail?"

Peering through the candlelight, Sarah saw the unspoken dig in her friend's wide eyes, saying louder than words, *So if you stick around here and marry him, you'll be able to see Lucy each and every day.*

"Would you enjoy that, Robbie?" Sarah asked, doubt in her voice.

"Would I!" he exclaimed to her amazement. "Lucy and Martin have the perfect life, Abigail. My sister is a very lucky woman." He grinned warmly at Martin. "What more could a woman want than an attentive husband, a handsome wardrobe, and teas and fittings with which to fill the day?"

"Intellectual stimulation?" Sarah asked innocently.

Robbie choked on a mouthful of roast turkey. "Excuse me," he apologized, wiping his mouth. "But you shouldn't jest so when a man's eating, Abigail. Do you think it's altogether fair to poke fun at the poor bluestockings who believe women are the equal of men?"

"Who's pok — "

"Abigail, my dear, now it's my brother's turn to tease *you!*" Lucy tittered. "He totally agrees with you that these females who don't know their places are a laughing matter."

"They are sad, though, aren't they, Lucy?" her husband asked, his homely, good-natured face sincere. "Why should a woman wish to come down off the pedestal upon which society has placed her unless she is a very confused soul?"

There was no use arguing, Sarah thought, exchanging a despairing look across the table with Micki. All these people saw things in a way that was as normal for the nineteenth century as it would have been ridiculous at the end of the twentieth. The Mannerings, the Shaws, the Bannisters weren't the strange ones. Sarah and Micki were.

She tried to imagine being back in Waterview and telling David Shaw she didn't want to know about his job at the Pizza Palace because "such things" as business didn't belong in her world. It was absurd. Even her sister Nicole, Sarah's immediate candidate for the most frivolous girl in their entire hometown, wouldn't find a life of needlepoint, sonnet-writing, and shopping ideal.

Looking around the table now, at the satisfied faces of the Southerners who couldn't help their own ignorance and who looked at things through the same lens as most people of their time, Sarah suddenly felt an intense longing to be at the table with all those she'd left behind.

So Nicole could be a pain. At least she wasn't a flighty flibbertigibbet like Lucy Bannister. And though Sarah had more than once accused her own brother of "macho manners above and beyond the call of duty," Simon would never laugh at Sarah's certainty that she was every bit his equal. She missed them terribly, she knew. And David, Aunt Pam, Heather, Tina, Matt, her mother and father, even Allison Rogers — how fabulous it would be to be sitting with people who would understand her, even if they wouldn't agree, any time she spoke her mind!

To hide the tears in her eyes, she paid great attention to the food on her plate, shutting out the gentle buzz of genteel Southern conversation that hummed beyond her ears. When she looked up and into Micki's eyes, she saw understanding and agreement, and she nodded to show Micki she now realized how the other girl had felt all along.

She smiled, hoping Micki got her signal that things were going to be all right. Somehow or another, she knew, she was going to get both of them home. She wasn't Abigail Mannering, although she'd almost let herself believe that she was. No, she was still Sarah Connell. And, equally important, she was still a witch. And since her being a witch was what got them into this, she was just going to have to make sure that it got them out.

Then, out of the flurry of conversation as plates were cleared and dessert was served, Sarah heard Mrs. Shaw's voice clearly, distinctly, over all the rest. "So," she was saying, "you will soon be going home?"

"Going home?" she blurted out. Had Robbie's mother somehow read her mind? And what did she know about Waterview?

"I was just saying to your cousin Delphinea" — Mrs. Shaw turned to Sarah — "she would soon be going home."

The girls exchanged looks of raw panic as Mr. Mannering answered for his houseguest. "Yes, Delphinea will be returning to Birmingham as scheduled next week."

"Next week?" Sarah gasped. "In just seven days?"

"The time has sped by for them," Mrs. Mannering explained to their hostess. "I'm sure neither our daughter nor our niece realized how soon their visit was drawing to a close."

Slowly, Sarah shook her head. Micki couldn't be leaving in just another week! What if she hadn't mastered her magical powers by then?

"I was just telling your mama that we would be happy to deliver your cousin safely home, Abigail," Martin Bannister told her. "And she agrees to allow you to accompany us and to spend the next two weeks at our home."

"You — you mean we'd take Delphinea to Birmingham and then I would go with you and Lucy to your home?"

"Isn't that a superb idea?" Lucy actually clapped her hands. "Oh, we'll have such fun, Abigail!"

"And I'm the one to miss all the merriment."

Robbie scowled with make-believe ferocity.

"It isn't our fault you'll be back with your regiment then," Lucy said primly. "Still, clever Robbie, I have no doubt you'll manage to finagle another brief leave to visit us while Abigail is in residence."

"A splendid idea!" Robbie smiled meaningfully at Sarah. "I couldn't have thought of a better one myself."

"That's settled then." Mr. Mannering looked pleased, as if he'd just done Sarah a favor condemning her to fourteen days of torture, Lucy-style, and perhaps to life in the Deep South forever.

And poor Micki! Even the warmth of the candleglow didn't brighten the suddenly bloodless tinge of Micki's skin.

"Don't worry," Sarah managed to whisper as she made sure she was the one to accompany Micki out of the room. "I'll get us out of here. And this time I mean it. By the time Abigail and Delphinea get into that carriage and hit the road, Micki and Sarah will have long since gone home!"

Chapter 14

"Don't look so sad, it's not as if you two are never going to see one another again!" Lucy Bannister's downright chipper tone was like salt in the wound of Sarah's pain. Silently, she gazed out the window as the countryside rolled by. Sarah saw nothing, however but the proof of her own foolishnes and the dangers of wishing for too many things.

"It's touching to see two cousins who are also such loving friends," Martin Bannister commended them, earning Micki's sad but grateful smile.

It wasn't touching, Sarah knew, and she didn't see how Micki could find it in her heart to still be a loving friend, not after the way Sarah had wrecked her life. Two weeks of Lucy's well-meaning if mindless chatter were

nothing compared to what poor Micki faced —
a return to "parents" she had yet to meet, too
many miles from Sarah to hope for another
chance of returning to Waterview for a long,
long time.

"I know why you're so blue, Abigail." Lucy,
thought Sarah, just didn't know when to zip
her lip. "Not only is your dear cousin being
taken away from you, but my brother has also
gone on his way."

"Now, Lucy, don't go on so. Abigail's affec-
tions are no one's business but her own."

And I don't believe I was willing to give up
my real friends and family for your brother,
Sarah felt like saying. He's nice, but let's face
it, Lucy-goosey, he's a real out-of-date sort of
guy.

Finally accepting that she wasn't going to
get a single word out of either passenger, Lucy
concentrated her attention on her doting husband, first assuring him that "Abigail was sure
to brighten up" once the three of them were
on their own.

And all Sarah could do was stare at the land-
scape, seeing nothing they passed by, aware
of nothing but the tightness in her chest and
the shame she felt at having gotten poor Micki
into this awful mess.

It was still difficult to believe she hadn't gotten both of them out. Her failure certainly wasn't for want of trying. The romance of the nineteenth century had worn off, and the harsh reality of life in the Confederacy was all that remained. But wish and worry though she might, Sarah had failed ten, twenty, thirty times in the past week to accomplish a thing. She hadn't managed to conjure up Aunt Pam or be an antenna, pulling in how-to-undo-your-own-wishes advice from out of the future. No matter what or when or where she wished, Sarah always opened her eyes to whatever had confronted her when she'd closed them. As Micki had finally exclaimed, laughing bravely through her tears the night before, "Frankly, my dear, we're gonna be whistling 'Dixie' till we've gummed our last grits."

The worst part was, Sarah knew she was doing *something* wrong. She had to be. She kept testing and retesting her powers. They'd weakened and couldn't be depended upon, occasionally failing as they had when she'd tried to use them to gather up the scattered skeins of embroidery floss that day in the morning room. How far away that day seemed now!

Still, more often than not, she could be counted upon to perform her feeble feats. But what good were those stupid tricks? So she could put things away, clean a room, wash dishes — who cared when a proper "lady" was expected to leave all the dirty work to the poor slaves? Who cared when everyone and everything you'd ever cared about was more than a thousand miles and a hundred years away?

Finally, both the Bannisters seemed to doze off and the inside of the carriage was quiet. Sarah glanced at Micki. Was she sleeping, too? At first Sarah thought so, then she noticed the fingers of Micki's right hand nervously plucking at the lace decorating her sleeves.

How did I get us here, Sarah asked herself one final time, and how can I get us out? Willing herself to stay calm and cool, she tried to picture exactly what she'd been thinking and doing back in that fateful history class. She remembered having trouble with the questions on the test and thinking how nice it would be if she and Micki and somebody like David could be down South before the Civil War.

She shook her head in frustration. There had to be something she was missing. If she could just picture —

"Maybe . . . just maybe," she murmured.

Even as Micki's eyes fluttered open at her voice, Sarah was sitting bolt upright in the carriage, shaking Lucy Bannister. "Lucy, please! Wake up!"

"Abigail? What is it?"

"What's wrong?"

Lucy and Martin were both awake and looking startled.

"Can we stop here, please? Just for a moment? I just want to spend a few moments alone with Cousin Delphinea, looking back on our beloved Georgia before we leave the state behind."

"Here?" Lucy peered from the carriage. "We're passing through the middle of a piney woods, Abigail."

"I'm sure Cousin Delphinea longs to remember the spicy scent of our Georgia pines when she's back in Birmingham," Sarah said sharply. "Please, Lucy, ask the driver to stop for a minute. Please?"

"That's little enough to ask," Martin Bannister said soothingly, reaching out through the window to bang on the side of the vehicle. "Whoa! Pull over for a spell, Ezra!" he called to the driver.

Sarah had the door open while the carriage wheels still slowly turned, and as soon as the horses stopped, she'd grabbed Micki's hand and was yanking her from the coach, turning to tell the stunned couple, "We'll be right back."

"What's going on?" Micki asked forlornly. "Sarah, where are we going?"

"To the twentieth century, if I have my way." Sarah's voice rang with a new determination.

"Why bother trying again? What's the use?"

"What've we got to lose?" Sarah asked sensibly. "This is it, Micki. Last chance. I may have stumbled on to the answer."

"You mean it?" Micki asked warily, as if afraid to hope.

"We'll find out soon enough. See, I was trying to figure out exactly how I'd gotten us here in the first place, Micki. I kept trying to picture myself in history class so I could reconstruct the scene of the crime."

"And?" Micki asked, breathless.

"And I kept thinking how I had to *picture* myself in history class and *picture* what I was doing. And then it came to me — I wasn't just wishing us back here, I was *picturing* us here. I didn't even realize it at the time, Micki, but the last thing that happened before I woke up in Abigail Mannering's bed was that I pictured you and me and somebody who looked like David Shaw all dressed in old-fashioned clothes."

"You think you can picture us back again?"

"It can't hurt to try, can it? Come on, Micki, just one last shot before I have to say goodbye to you in Birmingham. Please!"

The distant but unmistakable sound of Lucy's voice reached their ears. "Girls, y'all come back now, you hear? We've got to move on."

"Okay." Micki nodded tensely. "Tell me what to do, then hurry!"

"Just take my hand and close your eyes tight!" Sarah ordered. "Try to make your mind a blank. Or, better yet, try to see yourself as you were, back in history class."

Squeezing her eyes shut, Sarah made herself envision the interior of her classroom back at Waterview High. She saw herself, in her black-and-white outfit, bent over the history exam. Then, as if she were back in her own body, she made herself look down at the surface of the desk and see the examination paper.

"Abigail!" Faintly, she heard Lucy's voice, but she refused to open her eyes, refused to let the picture leave her as she wished with all her might that she and Micki could be in history class again.

"Lost in memories?" the voice asked, and Sarah's first thought was, Oh, no, couldn't that darned Lucy just stay in the stupid carriage?

Then she opened her eyes — and found herself staring up at Ms. Hines. In history class! In Waterview High! "Or do you just not know the answers to the questions?" the teacher went on.

"Oh, uh, no. I mean, I was just concentrating."

Nodding, Ms. Hines continued her walk down the aisle as Sarah heaved a sigh of relief. She was home again! Then, with a start, she remembered Micki. What if she'd left Micki back in the past?

But, no, there was Micki, scribbling notes at her desk. What's going on here? Frightened and confused, Sarah looked at the combination digital clock and calendar on the front wall. A mere matter of minutes had passed since the test began! It had all been a dream, of course! That was why Micki was scribbling away instead of slumped at her desk in a daze. Sarah chuckled. Wait until she told her Aunt Pam this one! She'd fallen asleep and actually thought she'd transported herself and Micki back through time!

Quickly, she bent to the task of finishing the test, finding now that the essay questions didn't seem nearly as hard as they had earlier.

As soon as the test papers were collected and the bell rang announcing the end of class, she hurried over to Micki. She couldn't wait to tell Micki about her daydream. *Delphinea*, she thought, giggling.

"Listen, you're not gonna believe — "

"We've got to have a serious talk as soon as possible," Micki interrupted huffily. "I mean it, Sarah, if you ever do something like that again, whether it's by accident or not — "

"What are you talking about, Micki?"

"Don't play dumb with me, *Abigail*. You're just lucky you managed to get us back here."

"You mean it wasn't a dream? It really did happen?"

Micki nodded. "Look." She opened her clenched fist. Clutched inside Sarah saw a piece of lace from the dress Delphinea had been wearing in the carriage. "I must have grabbed the end of my sleeve so tightly this tore off."

Sarah stared at the lace. "All that really happened? Poor Abigail and Delphinea! They must have wondered what in the world they were doing standing in the middle of the woods when Lucy finally got to them!"

"I'm glad you think it's so funny," Micki said as they walked out into the hallway. "I was terrified, Sarah!"

"So was I, Micki. Terrified." Coming toward them down the hall Sarah spotted David. "Wait here," she told Micki. "I'll be right back."

"David," Sarah said lightly, wondering how in the world she could manage to sound casual about what she was going to ask, "I was just wondering. . . . See, I was reading up on fashions from the Civil War and I seemed to recall someone mentioning, oh, at some time or another, that your great-great-great-grandfather had been a Confederate soldier. I, um, thought you might have one of his uniforms."

He shook his head. "Sorry."

"He wasn't a soldier?"

"Oh, he was a soldier. I just don't have any of his uniforms. Moths probably ate them all eons ago. Funny, I don't remember ever telling any of the kids I had a Confederate ancestor. Robert Shaw."

"What was his wife's name? Do you know?" she asked, sure he probably thought she'd stopped playing with a full deck.

"Sure, I know. My folks are very into family history and all that stuff. Abigail, that was her name. Matter of fact, my cousin Abby was named after her."

"So they got married!" Sarah exclaimed. Then, aware that David was peering at her as if she resembled something usually found in a petri dish, she said lamely, "Of course they did. Isn't that nice? And I'll bet they had a long and happy life, too. Those were the days!"

Still looking at her strangely, David shook his head. "No, to tell the truth, they didn't live happily ever after. Abigail was only, oh, maybe twenty when she died, right after she had her only baby, a son."

"She died?" Sarah whispered.

David nodded. "My dad's got this real old letter of Robert Shaw's, one that he wrote to his sister or someone. It talks about how Abigail got influenza and died. That sort of thing was really serious back in those days, you know. Yep, it got Abigail, and her cousin, too."

"I don't suppose you remember the cousin's name?"

David laughed. "You should be a reporter, Sarah! I don't remember what she was called. Something dopey, like Daffodil or Disneyland or Dentalwork."

"Delphinea," Sarah whispered under her breath.

"Oh, yeah! Listen, Sarah, we have a date Friday night, right? I have the night off."

Sarah said, "Wonderful, David," and hurried back up the hall to where she'd left Micki wait-

164

ing, murmuring under her breath as she trotted, "Delphinea and Abigail . . . Oh, to think that could have been us!"

"What were you talking to David about?" Micki asked when Sarah reached her. "You're white as a ghost."

"I'll tell you later, but who wouldn't be pale after a trip like that? Just think, Micki, we traveled a hundred years and back again. I sure am glad to be home," she confessed with a sigh of relief as she slipped her arm through her very best friend's. "I promise, from now on I'm going to be very, very careful!"

Sarah decided it was too early to tell her Aunt Pam what had happened. After all, if she told her aunt what she'd done, she might never learn how to do bigger and better things with her powers! Not that she wasn't going to keep her word to Micki and be very, very careful indeed.

As for those days of old when the Southern belle was in flower and all the folks down South were just waiting for Jefferson Davis to be inaugurated as President of the Confederate States so happy days could begin, well, those days never seemed very romantic to Sarah Connell again. If she even heard the slightest tinge of a drawl, she'd be overwhelmed by memories of tightly laced corsets, toe-pinching boots, and a life-style that was as cramped and uncomfortable as the clothing.

In fact, when she and David Shaw went out on their date on Friday night and he suggested catching a revival showing of *Gone With the Wind*, it was all Sarah could do not to faint and swoon and carry on.

She wondered if David would ever get over his shock when she insisted they go see some mindless third-rate *Star Wars* rip-off instead.

"I'll take the future over the past any day of the week, year, or century," Sarah told him, and she'd never been more sincere!

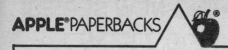

SUNFIRE®

Read all about the fascinating young women who lived and loved during America's most turbulent times!

☐ 32774-7		**AMANDA** Candice F. Ransom		**$2.95**
☐ 33064-0		**SUSANNAH** Candice F. Ransom		**$2.95**
☐ 33156-6		**DANIELLE** Vivian Schurfranz		**$2.95**
☐ 33241-4	#5	**JOANNA** Jane Claypool Miner		**$2.95**
☐ 33242-2	#6	**JESSICA** Mary Francis Shura		**$2.95**
☐ 33239-2	#7	**CAROLINE** Willo Davis Roberts		**$2.95**
☐ 33688-6	#14	**CASSIE** Vivian Schurfranz		**$2.95**
☐ 33686-X	#15	**ROXANNE** Jane Claypool Miner		**$2.95**
☐ 41468-2	#16	**MEGAN** Vivian Schurfranz		**$2.75**
☐ 41438-0	#17	**SABRINA** Candice F. Ransom		**$2.75**
☐ 42134-4	#18	**VERONICA** Jane Claypool Miner		**$2.75**
☐ 40049-5	#19	**NICOLE** Candice F. Ransom		**$2.25**
☐ 42228-6	#20	**JULIE** Vivian Schurfranz		**$2.75**
☐ 40394-X	#21	**RACHEL** Vivian Schurfranz		**$2.50**
☐ 40395-8	#22	**COREY** Jane Claypool Miner		**$2.50**
☐ 40717-1	#23	**HEATHER** Vivian Schurfranz		**$2.50**
☐ 40716-3	#24	**GABRIELLE** Mary Francis Shura		**$2.50**
☐ 41000-8	#25	**MERRIE** Vivian Schurfranz		**$2.75**
☐ 41012-1	#26	**NORA** Jeffie Ross Gordon		**$2.75**
☐ 41191-8	#27	**MARGARET** Jane Claypool Miner		**$2.75**
☐ 41207-8	#28	**JOSIE** Vivian Schurfranz		**$2.75**
☐ 41416-X	#29	**DIANA** Mary Francis Shura		**$2.75**
☐ 42043-7	#30	**RENEE** Vivian Schurfranz (February '89)		**$2.75**

Scholastic Inc., P.O. Box 7502, 2932 East McCarty Street, Jefferson City, MO 65102

Please send me the books I have checked above. I am enclosing $ _____
(please add $1.00 to cover shipping and handling). Send check or money-order—no cash or C.O.D.'s please.

Name _____

Address _____

City _____ State/Zip _____

Please allow four to six weeks for delivery. Offer good in U.S.A. only. Sorry, mail order not available to residents of Canada. Prices subject to change.   **SUN 888**